PIG TALES

Marie Darrieussecq was born in 1969 in Bayonne, France, a town renowned for its ham, and is a graduate of the Ecole Normale Supérieure in Paris. *Pig Tales*, her first novel, was published in France in 1996 and became a great international success. Her second novel, *My Phantom Husband*, appeared in 1998, followed by *Breathing Underwater* in 2001, and *A Brief Stay with the Living* in 2003.

Acclaim for *My Phantom Husband*:

'An extraordinarily good second novel . . . That Darrieussecq can sustain this lonely, existential voice in the face of such all-encompassing uncertainty is a massive achievement; one that recalls, in literary terms, the nihilism of Beckett or Camus.' Alex Clark, *Guardian*

'Darrieussecq is as daring as she is original and politically astute. This new book is a remarkable achievement . . . It looks like French fiction has found a saviour; it has certainly discovered a singular new voice.' Eileen Battersby, *Irish Times*

Acclaim for *Breathing Underwater*:
'There are very few writers who may have changed my perception of the world, but Darrieussecq is one of them.' Francis Gilbert, *The Times*

'A perfect example of her singular style: both lucid and opaque, ambiguous and utterly defining . . . [She] is at the height of her powers; complex and deliberately, maddeningly, mysterious, she is not always easy, and in that lies her brilliance: her gifts are dazzling.' Nicola McAllister, *Observer*

MARIE DARRIEUSSECQ

Pig Tales

A Novel of Lust and Transformation

Translated from the French
by Linda Coverdale

faber and faber

First published in France as *Truismes* in 1996 by Editions P.O.L
First published in the USA as *Pig Tales* in 1997
by The New Press
Published simultaneously in Great Britain
by Faber and Faber Limited
3 Queen Square London WC1N 3AU
This paperback edition first published in 2003

Typeset by Faber and Faber Ltd
Printed in England by Mackays of Chatham plc, Chatham, Kent

A CIP record for this book
is available from the British Library

ISBN 0–571–19372–2

4 6 8 10 9 7 5 3

Then the knife plunges in. The farmhand gives it two little shoves to push it through the thick skin, after which the long blade seems to melt through the neck fat as it sinks in up to the hilt.

At first the boar doesn't understand a thing, he remains stretched out for a few seconds, thinking about it. Aha! Then he realizes he is being killed and utters strangled cries until he can scream no more.

Knut Hamsun

I know how much this story might upset people, how much distress and confusion it could cause. I suspect that any publisher who agrees to take on this manuscript will be heading for trouble – heading for prison, probably – and I'd like to apologize right now for the inconvenience. But I must write this book without further delay, because if they find me in my present state, no one will listen to me or believe what I say. Simply holding a pen gives me terrible cramps. I haven't enough light, either, so I have to stop at nightfall, and I write very, very slowly. I won't tell you about the problems I had getting this notebook or about the mud, which dirties everything and dilutes ink that's barely dry. I hope that any publisher patient enough to decipher these piggle-squiggles will graciously take into consideration the enormous effort I'm making to write as legibly as possible. Even the act of remembering is quite difficult for me. But if I concentrate hard and try to think back as far as I can, back to right before the events recounted here, I manage to recover some images. I must admit that my new way of life, the frugal diet I follow, these rustic accommodations that suit me perfectly, and my astonishing ability to withstand cold (something I've noticed as winter draws on) are good reasons why I don't miss the more painful aspects of my former life. I remember that I was out of work when it all began, and that looking for a job depressed me in ways I no longer understand. I entreat the reader, especially the unemployed reader, to pardon the impropriety of my words. Unfortunately, however, there will be a great deal more impropriety in this book, and I beg all those whom it might shock to please forgive me.

So I was looking for work. I had interviews. And got nowhere. Until I filled out a *job application form* (words are coming back to me) for a big perfume and cosmetics chain. The director of the firm sat me on his lap and pawed at my right breast, obviously finding it marvellously elastic. At that point in my life, men in general had begun finding me marvellously elastic. I'd put on weight – four or five pounds, perhaps – because I'd started feeling constantly hungry, and I could see in the mirror that those pounds had distributed themselves nicely around my figure. Without sports, without any particular exercise, my flesh had become firmer, smoother, plumper than before. Now I understand that this extra weight and the wonderful quality of my flesh must have been the very first symptoms. The director of Perfumes Plus was holding my right breast in one hand, the job contract in the other. I could feel my breast heaving with the emotion of seeing that contract so close to being signed, but also with that – how shall I put it – *pneumatic* aspect my flesh had acquired. The director told me that in the boutique the important thing was to look lovely and well groomed at all times. He was sure I would approve of the employees' uniforms, which were tight fitting and would look quite attractive on me. His fingers moved a little lower and were unbuttoning anything there was to unbutton, an activity that naturally obliged him to put the contract down on his desk. I read and reread it over his shoulder: part-time employment paying almost the minimum wage, which would allow me to contribute to the rent at home and buy myself a dress or two. And the contract specifically said that during the annual inventory clearance, I would be entitled to some cosmetics. I'd have a chance at getting the most famous brands, the most expensive perfumes! The director had me get down on my knees in front of him, and while I was hard at work, I daydreamed about these beauty preparations, about how good I was going to smell, about the glowing complexion I'd have. Honoré would undoubtedly find me even more alluring. I'd met Honoré on the day I dug my old bathing suit out of the closet for the fifth spring in a row. It was while trying on the suit that I'd noticed my thighs had grown pink and firm, curvaceous, yet muscular. I was filling out from all that eating. So I'd treated myself to an afternoon at Aqualand. It was raining outside, but at Aqualand it was always warm and pleasant. Going to Aqualand cost almost a tenth of my monthly unemployment cheque, and my mother hadn't approved of my outing at all. She'd even refused to give me a Métro ticket, and to get through the turnstile I was forced to squeeze up against some man. There are always lots of them waiting around for girls at the Métro turnstiles. I definitely felt that I'd made an impression on the gentleman – bluntly put, much more of an impression than I usually made. I had to wash my skirt discreetly in one of the changing rooms at Aqualand. You should always be careful there to make sure the doors are completely closed, and you must know how to make yourself scarce when the room is already occupied by a couple, because gentlemen are always lounging around there, too, in front of the doors on the women's side. You can earn a good living at Aqualand, but I'd never gone in for that, even when my mother was threatening to throw me out of the house. In the empty changing room I slipped hurriedly out of my clothes and into my bathing suit, and once again, in the flattering reflection of the gilded mirror, I thought I looked – forgive me for saying so – incredibly gorgeous, like a fashion model, but more voluptuous. I washed myself with some free scented soaps. The door opened but it was only a few women coming in, no men, so we were able to relax in relative peace. The women laughed as they undressed. They were a group of rich Muslims who put on very long, luxurious bathing dresses that clung to their bodies in translucent veils beneath the showers. Gathering around me, the women made a fuss over my beauty and gave me a sample bottle of fancy perfume, as well as a few coins. I felt safe with them. Aqualand is a place where you can take it easy, but you still have to watch out for yourself. That's why when Honoré came over to me in the water, my first reaction was to flee. I swam off with a vigorous crawl, and perhaps that's what attracted him the most (I was a good swimmer at the time). But when he offered me a drink in the tropical bar afterwards, I saw right away that he was okay. There we were, the two of us, dripping all over the bar, sweating in our wet bathing suits, with a big black guy fanning us, and I could see in all the mirrors on the ceiling that I was flushed bright red. We were drinking super-sweet, super-colourful cocktails, there was calypso music, and all of a sudden we were worlds away. The wave machine was churning out big ones. Honoré was telling me that sharks were put in the pool for certain private receptions, and before the fresh water killed them, they had five minutes in which to snap up the slowest guests. This created, it seems, a unique ambience at the festivities. Then everyone would swim in the red water until the wee hours. Honoré was a teacher in a big suburban junior high school. Private parties disgusted him. He never even went to his students' celebrations. Me, I would have liked to be a student, I said to him, and he told me absolutely not: students were all rotten and depraved, so he came to Aqualand to meet wholesome girls. We hit it off together. He asked me if I ever went to private receptions. I said never; I didn't know anyone. He told me he'd introduce me to people. In the beginning that's what intrigued me: the fact that this guy, besides being polite, was offering to help me make friends, but in reality Honoré didn't have any himself, couldn't manage to make any in spite of his job, and was perhaps hoping, thanks to me, to get invited to the *in* places. On our way out, Honoré bought me a dress in one of the elegant shops of Aqualand: a dress of transparent lazuré that I never wore for anyone but him. We made love for the first time in the dressing room of that trendy boutique. I saw myself in the mirror, saw Honoré's hands on my back, his fingers carving elastic furrows deep in my skin. He had never, Honoré panted, ever met such a wholesome girl before. The Muslim women had come into the store, you could hear them chattering in their language. Honoré kept looking at me while he got dressed again; I was stark naked, and felt a

6

touch chilly. The saleslady offered us mint tea and cook-
ies, which she passed under our dressing room door. She
was discreet and quite nice. I thought I might like having that kind of job. As it turned out, my work at
Perfumes Plus wasn't that much different. The chain
sold all kinds of fragrances you had to try out on various
parts of the body to see if the scent would develop well
or not, which took time, so there was a different dressing
room for each scent. I'd settle the ladies on the big sofas
in the rooms and explain to them, the way I was supposed to, that only a relaxed body could release the full
palette of a perfume. (I'd taken a training course to be a
masseuse.) I handed out Prozac and extracts of swan's
down. It wasn't an unpleasant profession. Still, when
the Muslim women had gone, after charging about five
thousand euros on their Internet cards, this *très chic*
saleslady sprayed some perfume all through the store,
before our very eyes. I would never, I told Honoré, ever
allow myself to be guilty of such bad taste if I ran a high-
class boutique. That's when Honoré said that with a
body like mine and such a blooming appearance, I
would get all the ritzy boutiques I wanted. He turned
out to be right, in the end. But he didn't want me to
work. He said work corrupted women. I was disappointed to discover, however, that despite his pres-
tigious profession, his salary allowed him to rent

nothing better than a lousy one-bedroom apartment in a nearby suburb. I told myself immediately that it was only fair that I get my rear in gear and help him out.

It was around then, during my first days at Perfumes Plus, that our female clients began to tell me I had a marvellous complexion. The boutique started doing a bang-up business with me on board. The director congratulated me. It's true that the work uniform, a sober white smock like the ones beauticians wear, was most becoming, quite close fitting, cut extremely low both in the front and the back. Now, at that same time, my breasts began to become as shapely as my thighs. It had got to the point where I'd had to abandon my B cups, and the wire supports in my bras were killing me. I hadn't received my first pay cheque yet, just a tiny advance, because all the computers were down in the accounting department, so I couldn't buy myself a C cup. The director reassured me, however, saying that I didn't need a bra at all, that at my age they held up fine on their own. And it's true that they held up remarkably well, even when I hit size D, but that's when I gave in and bought a bra with what I'd managed to set aside from the grocery money. Honoré asked me questions about that; he knew I hadn't been paid yet, but I carried it off without admitting a thing, even though that little betrayal still bothers me. Poor Honoré, he couldn't possibly know what it's like to run braless after a bus when you're that big. I was getting more and more male clients at the boutique, and they paid well. The director came by almost every day to pick up the money, and he was increasingly pleased with me. My massages were a great hit, and I even believe that the director suspected that I'd moved along to the special massages on my own initiative, whereas normally management waited awhile before suggesting this to the salesgirls. After a few weeks, thanks to all this money, I was in no danger of getting fired. The director didn't push me into doing anything; it all happened with the utmost discretion. The director was great. He left me alone for quite a while, probably figuring I was tired from all this work. Well, I'd never felt better in my life. And this had nothing to do with Honoré. It had nothing to do with my new job, either – although I liked it a lot – or even with the money, since in any case I didn't get that until much later and even then only some of it, and it would never have been enough to make me independent. No, it was just that I was always in a sunny mood, as it were, even in the Métro, even throughout that muddy spring, even in the dusty public squares where I'd go to eat my sandwich at noon. And yet it wasn't such an easy life, objectively speaking. I had to get up early, but strangely enough, at cockcrow – or whatever its urban equivalent would be – I woke up easily, on my own, without needing any pep pills in the morning or sleeping pills at night, whereas Honoré and everyone around me kept popping them like sweets. Another thing that was inconvenient was that I'd be hungry when I'd get to my little park, truly ravenous, but I never had time to relax while I ate. The air, the birds – I don't know, whatever nature was left – really affected me all of a sudden. 'It's spring,' my girlfriends said, to tease me. They were jealous of Honoré, envious at seeing me so beautiful, yet flattered that with all this success I would still call them occasionally. And then, well, sometimes the clients weren't that much fun. I had fewer and fewer women – I think they were frightened off by the weird atmosphere in the boutique. Sometimes customers tried things I didn't like, and ordinarily that would have depressed me, but at the time I was as happy as a lark. The clientele loved me. They all said I was extraordinarily wholesome. I was becoming proud, proud of myself, I mean. But that wasn't it, either. The thing that was giving me such terrific morale was the exciting impression of starting a new life. One of my last remaining female clients, a regular who was a real character, she opened my eyes. She was a shaman, in everyday life, and fantastically rich. I was busy massaging her when she announced

that it was probably hormonal. I repeated what my
friends had said about spring fever, but the woman was
adamant. 'No, no,' she told me, 'it comes from you, from
inside you. Are you sure you're not pregnant?' That was
the month that my periods stopped. This thought left
me, in a word, speechless. I didn't say anything to
Honoré. The client was rather old, she knew a lot about
life, and I liked her. She was one of those women who
always want to chat during the massage, I think she was
– what's the word here – frigid. It must have pleased her
to see me looking so lovely, so young, so healthy, as
everyone said, and knowing that I was pregnant must
have excited her even more, I don't know quite how to
put it. There are fewer and fewer babies around. Me, I
have nothing against babies. I used to see some in the little park now and then. In any case, my appetite kept getting bigger, and this client recognized a slew of
symptoms. 'Do you have any cravings?' she asked me.
Now she was coming in daily for a massage – the male
customers were furious, they called her the old hag. I
didn't have cravings, I had revulsions instead. 'Same
thing,' she told me, and demanded details. I couldn't eat
ham sandwiches any more, they made me sick, and once
I even threw up in the park. Not very classy. Luckily it
was too early in the day for the clients or the director to
see me. I switched to chicken right away, it sat better

with me. 'You see,' the woman said, 'you have cravings for chicken: well, with my first son I couldn't stand pork – anyway when you're pregnant, you must definitely avoid pork because of diseases.' I knew she'd never had any children, and a male customer had told me she was a lesbian, it was *absolutely obvious*. My periods still hadn't returned. I kept getting hungrier, and to vary my meals I'd bring hard-boiled eggs, some chocolate. It was hard to find fresh vegetables at an affordable price, so I'd asked a client to bring me some from his house in the country, and he brought me apples as well. You should have seen me eat those apples. I never had enough time to munch them properly, really chew them – my mouth would be bursting with juice, my teeth crunching up the flesh – and the taste! My few moments of leisure, off in the little park with my apples, surrounded by birds, were just about the joy of my life. I longed for green things, for nature. I let myself be persuaded to spend a weekend at this client's country place and pretended I was taking a training course so Honoré wouldn't say anything. I was sorely disappointed. The house was charming, set among trees, isolated, with countryside all around; I'd never seen anything like it. But I spent the entire weekend inside, as the client had invited some of his friends. Through the window I could see fields, thickets, and I had the most – how can I describe it –

intense desire to go stick my nose into everything, roll around on the grass, sniff it, nibble it. But the client kept me tied up the whole weekend. I could have just cried when we drove back. I didn't want to service him any more in the car, and besides, it's dangerous on the highway, and that son of a bitch dumped me on the outskirts of the city, without any consideration, and he never came back to the boutique. I lost a good customer. When I got back home I started bleeding. I had terrible pains in my abdomen and could barely walk. Honoré said women always have problems with their insides. He was sweet, he paid for me to go see a gynaecologist. The gynaecologist was in a huge hurry. He told me that I'd had a miscarriage, stuffed me full of gauze, and sent me off to a clinic. It was very expensive, the curettage. But personally, I'm certain I wasn't pregnant. I don't know what got into me all of a sudden to make me argue with the gynaecologist about this – anyway he became furious and called me a little slut. I didn't dare tell him what had happened with the client and his friends. They put me through a lot of pain at the clinic, and all for nothing, I swear. It seems to me you know when you're pregnant. You must smell it on your body, a kind of odour of maternity, and although I'd become extremely sensitive to odours, I didn't smell anything like that on my skin. Besides, I'm convinced that except for my female client –

who was a little queer – the customers would have avoided me if they'd guessed I was pregnant. They loved me healthy, but not to that extent. My belly still aches a bit, even now, from everything they did to me at the clinic. I was still a female when it was all over, though. And the reason why to this day I continue to say I wasn't pregnant is that almost immediately after that supposed miscarriage my periods stopped again, and the same symptoms – the hunger, the nausea, the pudginess – continued as before. In spite of these few annoyances (unless they were all part of one big annoyance), I was still in excellent spirits. The elderly client loved me more than ever. She kept at it, touching my belly, pointing it out to me in the mirror, and my stomach was getting quite round, too – too round, if you had asked me. But the clients continued to find me terribly sexy, that's all that mattered. They even stood in line. The elderly client spent a great deal of time with me. She was the last woman who still came to the boutique and my only confidante, in a way, because my *radiance*, as she described it, had sort of discouraged all my female friends. I liked chatting with the old woman, I didn't find her body offensive, and it interested me to see what I was going to look like in a few years. Was I ever wrong. She offered me dresses of hers that were still wearable, and even a piece of jewellery she didn't care for any more. The old woman was murdered. One day she didn't show up and they found her body in the square, under a tree. Not a pretty sight, it seems. After that I often noticed one of her friends, a woman dressed all in black, who came to cry beneath the trees in the little park. It's wonderful to have friends like that. As for me, I no longer had the old woman to talk to, so I was on my own about that problem with my periods. In a way, it was a relief not to see her any more, because I knew perfectly well that I wasn't pregnant, that she was the one who wanted me to be, and she'd been getting me all confused. At least the male clients weren't preoccupied with that sort of thing, they didn't look at me to see how I was. In fact they were preoccupied with themselves, it made them feel good to be able to feel me up. Their kind of indifference suited me, actually, because I thought that I was getting a mite too tubby and that this chubbiness was no longer as appealing as before, but since I received only regular customers at the boutique, I didn't have to be afraid that newcomers might see me as I really was, so to speak. All my clients knew that I was to their liking, that was enough for them, and they weren't going to look any further. In any case, a change in my appearance would have seemed *incongruous* to them, I believe that's the word. (It was later on that I figured all this out.) I was beginning to know them pretty well, my customers, especially since my part-time job had gradually become full time in order to accommodate everyone. I would get these strange ideas, ideas I'd never had before, I can say that now. I began to judge my clientele. I even had preferences. I watched some of them arrive with real distaste, which I managed to hide, luckily. Furthermore, I think all these new ideas were related to the absence of menstruation. Even though I still maintained that curious good humour, that robust health, I was finding it harder and harder to put up with some of my clients' whims. You might say that I had an opinion on everything. I kept quiet, of course, and I submitted, that's what I was paid to do, but I felt that my body wasn't going along any more, my non-menstruating body. It's my body that controls my head – I know that only too well now – and I've paid dearly, even if I'm basically glad to be through with the customers. But at the time, I thought you could do as you pleased without your body having to pay the price. And everything seemed fine, too. It was only after I put on a little too much weight – and even before the customers noticed it – that I began to disgust myself. I'd look in the mirror and see actual folds at my waist, almost rolls of flesh! Now I smile at the memory. I tried to cut down on the sandwiches, I even managed to stop eating at noon, but I kept getting bigger. I was haunted by the models in the photos at the boutique. I was convinced that my entire body was affected by some kind of freakish retention of blood. My complexion was turning ruddy, and the customers gradually fell into barnyard ways with me. Too engrossed in themselves and their pleasure, they never noticed a thing, but their new inclinations turned the massage table into a sort of haystack out in a field. Some of the clients began to bray, others grunted like pigs, and little by little, most of them wound up on all fours. I told myself that if my periods finally returned, all that blood would empty out of me and I'd become as dainty as a girl once more. I had these cravings for bloodlettings. The clients themselves were getting fatter. My knees ached beneath their weight. I was seeing stars, I was seeing knives, cleavers. I bought more and more sophisticated electrical appliances for the kitchen, and Honoré was pleased by these new domestic penchants. In the end I simply had to admit the obvious. Since I'd started thinking about everything, having ideas about everything, I couldn't rationally close my eyes any more to my condition and deny that I was pregnant. I'd gained more than thirteen pounds in one month, especially on my breasts, stomach, thighs; I had big red cheeks, almost like a mask, and a hunger that wouldn't quit. At night I was having bizarre dreams about blood, about sausages, and I'd get up to vomit. I'm ashamed even now of those preposterous dreams, but that's what was happening. I'd try to understand, and sometimes I'd have strange flashes of lucidity, a gut feeling of certainty. It scared me. Being pregnant was in a sense the only objective and rational connection among all these symptoms. Honoré wanted me to stop working; he was suspicious and must have known something was going on. Aside from that, he was rather proud of me, curiously enough. My boutique was the talk of the entire capital, it was all the rage, and celebrities flocked to see me. Honoré couldn't help noticing the economic dividends as well – all that kitchen gadgetry, for example. And then he couldn't complain, I was coming home every evening, apart from a few weekends. I'd decided not to tell him anything because if he'd known I was pregnant, he would have done everything possible to keep me at home. For three months I would have received pre-maternity benefits that were much higher than my salary (I was still on the part-time payroll), and after that I would've been stuck with Honoré. I wanted to keep my job, I don't quite know why, really. It was like a window, I could see the park, the birds. In any case, if they'd known I was pregnant I'd have been fired. How could I tell the director of Perfumes Plus? It was unthinkable. He'd have accused me of being careless, but I wasn't earning enough to be able to be careful, and Honoré always thought it was up to women to deal with that female stuff. So that's another reason why I believed I was pregnant, because I wasn't being careful. There is a certain biological logic, after all, even if the least I can say at the moment is that I have my doubts about it. Well, my only asset was my *pneumatic* aspect, and I must admit that I was slowly losing it. Another month or two and I wouldn't be able to get into my uniform at all: my belly was huge, while the shoulder straps and décolletage were already less exciting now that my flesh was bulging out too much. At our first inventory clearance, after I'd been on the job exactly one year, I got some face powder that I patted on every morning, which slightly toned down my apple-cheeked peasant look. I was able to hang on for another month. But I was gaining weight all over, not just around the belly. And my belly didn't look at all like that of a pregnant woman: what I had wasn't a nice round globe, but rolls of fat. I mean I'd seen pregnant women before, I knew what they looked like. It hadn't been all that long since my own mother had waited until the fifth month before tearfully getting an abortion, as we couldn't do without her salary at home. I was hardly eating anything now. I had dizzy spells during the day, absurd dreams every night. Honoré said my grunting bothered him, then it was my squealing; when he wouldn't sleep with me any more, I slept in the living room. It was better for both of us, since I could sprawl comfortably on my side and snore. I was sleeping more and more badly, though, and I tried to disguise the bags under my eyes with Yerling Cover Up Creme – two free tubes I'd received as a New Year's gift – but the makeup was too old and crumbly. I really looked awful. I was having horrible anxiety attacks at the idea of this abortion. Women who have abortions aren't treated with kid gloves. It's even said that doctors don't bother with anaesthetic for women like that – who should just learn to be more careful! And then there are always those militant crusaders to be afraid of. At the time I wasn't keeping up with the news, so I wasn't too clear about them. Now I'm well away from all that, fortunately. I went to the clinic. I'd sold some ultra-chic lipsticks under the counter and I was terrified of getting caught. I stayed only six hours, but the director of Perfumes Plus did not at all appreciate my bunking off half a day like that. There was a guy chained to the stirrups of the operating table, chanting something, but this jerk had chained himself too low and wasn't actually in the way. He had to be there for everything, and by the time the police arrived to cut his chains – since he'd swallowed the key – he was drenched in my blood. At the clinic they told him he wouldn't last long if he kept on swallowing keys. They told me that if I wasn't more careful, I risked becoming

sterile after my two curettages. They also told me
they'd never seen such an oddly shaped uterus, and I'd
be well advised to be concerned about it since there
were lots of diseases around. They even kept the hys-
terography for closer study. The protestor accompanied
me back to the boutique. He was livid. He told me I was
damned for ever, that I had no idea – unhappy girl that
I was – of the consequences of my act, and he called me
a lost soul. I couldn't have cared less about what he was
saying, I was leaning on his arm to get back to the store.
He was nice, basically – I'd never have been able to
walk without him. I wondered how I was going to manage to deal with the clients and keep from getting blood
everywhere. I raised the metal shutter, and when the
guy saw the shop sign, he went even whiter. Stepping
back, he pointed his index and little fingers at me, saying I was a creature of the devil. 'There it is!' he
shouted. Then he stared, sort of studying me. 'The mark
of the Beast!' he yelled. Well, I was kind of upset, that
someone could look at me and say that. The guy ran off.
I checked myself in the mirror. I didn't see anything
unusual. For once I was pale instead of looking like a
red-faced farm girl. That bloodletting had done me
some good after all.

I returned to work with a light heart, no longer worried

about whether I was pregnant. The clients were still paying well. The boss was highly pleased with me and let me have a slightly bigger percentage, saying that I was his best worker. At the next inventory clearance, at a ceremony held before all the other saleswomen of the chain and some VIPs, I was awarded a medal, a Moonlight Madness compact, and a selection of Gilda skin creams with *suractivated DNA for cellular renewal and macromolecular recombination*. They were brand-new products. I wept for joy at the ceremony. They took pictures. I was very proud, you could see that in the photos. You could also see that I'd got fatter, but not as much as all that because ever since the abortion I'd had increasingly frequent bouts of nausea and I'd lost some weight. You couldn't blame that on pregnancy any more. Something was wrong. I had to be more and more careful with my diet and was hardly eating anything besides vegetables, mostly potatoes, which were what I digested best. I'd become crazy about raw potatoes, unpeeled, I should add. Honoré was somewhat put off by this. Now he was really wondering if I was pregnant. But in spite of his rather disgusted attitude, Honoré did not like to be kept waiting. He had to have it every evening, now, and I didn't even have time to freshen up before I was expected to put out for him. It was just like it was with the customers. There I'd been, thinking my love handles would offend them – well, not one bit. Amazingly, they all seemed to like me kind of fat, even the new ones, who were fitted into my already overcrowded schedule by special dispensation from the director, since they paid well. Their desire turned bestial, so to speak. The sessions had scarcely begun when they wanted everything, right away: the special package and the Hi-Tech *prix fixe* with the oils and the vibrator and all (and this stuff wasn't cheap), but I could see they didn't give a hoot about the oils whereas they were snatching the vibrator out of my hands – and doing some pretty kinky things with it, I'm telling you. I'd come out of there exhausted. Women are more refined, at least. All my former female customers used to adore the Hi-Tech number, they couldn't get enough of it. I was beginning to regret having an exclusively male clientele. I was selling fewer and fewer perfumes and creams, but the director didn't seem to care. Supplies were accumulating in my stockroom and I'd already picked out the ones I was going to keep for myself at our next inventory clearance. It wasn't a bad line of work. There were some satisfactions, after all. When they'd got their money's worth, the male clients always had a few kind words for me; they found me *ravishing*, and sometimes they used other words I wouldn't dare write but which pleased me just as much, actually. I could see that I was exactly like they said, all I had to do was look in the mirror, I wasn't an idiot. My finest feature was now my derrière. It stretched my uniform to bursting – sometimes I even had to mend the seams, but the director refused to let me buy a larger one on credit. He said the chain was on the brink of disaster, that there wasn't any money. We salesgirls made big financial sacrifices, fearing that the firm would go under and we'd lose our jobs. My few co-workers – whom I rarely saw – always told me how well off I was, having an honest man like Honoré to support me in a pinch. They were jealous, especially of my derrière. What they didn't mention was that most of them kept for themselves money that the customers gave them. Me, I never did this, one has one's pride after all. I didn't much want to see my fellow salesgirls – they weren't high class, to say the least. My clients knew there was no question of money between us, that everything went directly to the chain and that I received my percentage, nothing more. I was proud of having the soundest accounts in the entire firm. The other salesgirls badmouthed me. They took big risks as far as the director was concerned, too. They were lucky I didn't rat on them, because the director had his own ways of dealing with dishonest girls. Besides, in the end there was always some disgruntled customer to blow the whistle and then take part in the re-education session. Me, I did my work properly. Everything in my boutique was open and above board. I accepted compliments and bouquets of flowers. That's all. But what I find difficult to admit here – and yet I'll have to get this out because I realize now that it was one of the symptoms – is that, well, I used to eat these flowers. I'd go in the back of the shop, put them in a vase, and look at them for quite a while. Then I'd eat them. It was their fragrance, probably. It went to my head, all that greenery, and the sight of so many colours. It was nature outside coming inside the boutique, and it stirred something in me. I was ashamed, especially since the bouquets cost so much – I knew it was an extravagance for the clients to bring me flowers. So I'd always try to keep one or two blossoms to put in my buttonhole. That required true self-control: in a way, it was a little personal victory. The clients enjoyed seeing their flowers nestled against my breasts. And what reassured me was that they ate the flowers, too. They'd lean over me and snip! They'd pluck them from my décolletage with one bite, then chew them with a greedy air and a come-hither look. In general I found my clients charming, cute as could be. They were growing increasingly interested in my derrière, that was the only problem. What I mean is – and I urge all sensitive souls not to read this page, for their own self-respect – that my customers had some peculiar predilections, some completely unnatural ideas, if you follow me. The first times, I told myself that after all, if the chain could earn some extra money thanks to me, I should be eager to do anything to help things go even better. But I wasn't really sure at what point the clients were beginning to go too far: I didn't know, exactly, where I had to draw the line to safeguard public morals. It took some time and courage for me to dare confide in the director about this. To my surprise, he laughed heartily and called me a *little girl*, and I was moved to tears by what I felt was a certain affection in his words. The director even gave me a special cream from Yerling to soften and moisturize those sensitive areas, and with that I burst out sobbing. The director must have been truly pleased with me to have showered me with so much kindness. Then he was patient enough to take the time to perfect my training. After drying my tears, he had me sit on him and he shoved something up my rear end. That hurt even more than with the clients, but he told me it was for my own good, everything would be fine afterwards, and I wouldn't have any more problems. I bled a lot, but you couldn't call it a period. My periods hadn't returned after my abortion. The director told me always to be very polite with the customers. Then something curious and absolutely unseemly happened, and once again I beg any impressionable readers to skip these pages. Bluntly put, I began really wanting sex. Outwardly, nothing was different: the customers were the same, and Honoré as well, and this change hadn't anything to do with the additional training granted to me by the director, either. But while the clients were now focusing greedily and exclusively on my backside, I would personally have preferred that they direct their interest in me elsewhere. I did gymnastics in secret to reduce my buttocks, I even took an aerobics class, but I couldn't manage to reduce my rear end. On the contrary, I gained even more weight there. It was the centre of everyone's attention. So, in order to entice the customers' eyes elsewhere, I let my uniform split open at the bust, and I seized the initiative. The first time I sat astride a customer, it didn't work out at all. He called me names I won't dare repeat here. I realized that it wasn't going to be easy to take the initiative away from the customers, which meant it wasn't going to be easy to get what I wanted. So I took my cue from the movies. I began teasing and flirting. It drove the customers crazy. Before, I'd behaved impeccably, in a manner befitting an upscale boutique, not allowing myself the slightest lapse in taste. But when I started becoming involved in my work – and it pains me to say this – the customers began carrying on like dogs. Although I did lose a few who seemed to miss the former style of the establishment and were unable to weather the change.

But I wanted it too badly, you understand. In the beginning I was afraid of losing too many clients, afraid our earnings would drop off. To my amazement, however, I picked up a new kind of clientele, doubtless by word of mouth. These new customers appeared to be seeking a salesgirl like me, really keen, someone who put herself out and so on, I'll spare you the details. Later I discovered that I'd encroached upon the clientele of certain other boutiques in the chain, which created some confusion, and the director asked me in no uncertain terms to calm down. He even slapped me when I asked him if he wanted to take advantage of my services. He'd never been shy about that before, though. The clients I now preferred were those who asked me to tie them up for their massage. That did something to me. I could do as I pleased. I thought I looked beautiful in the mirrors: somewhat flushed, true, a little chunky, but savage – I don't know quite how to put it. You could see something like pride in my eyes and in my body. When I was through, the customers looked wild-eyed as well. You'd have thought you were in the jungle. Some of the clients were so exuberant I could have eaten them right up. And the ones who clung to their former ways, those who hadn't yet understood that the house style had changed, those who still wanted the timid, blushing stuff, and a bit of bottom, well I put them in their place but good. I got knocked around, especially by those who'd already been used to hitting me before getting their special massage. But I didn't care. Something so extraordinary was happening in me that even the refresher course the director put me through wrung only a few cries from me. He now found me too forward, too coarse: there was no room in the firm for *bitches in heat*. Customers had complained. By taking me off for a long weekend with his treasurer and his Dobermans, the director thought he'd cured me for ever of my taste for fooling around. He thought our former clients would be able once again to put a well-behaved, docile, demure *little girl* through her paces without hearing a single peep from her. Well, he was wrong. What was astounding was that I liked it now, I mean, not only the massages you can advertise in the shop window and the product demonstrations, no – all the rest of it, at least what I undertook on my own. Of course there were still clients who cherished the old ways. I couldn't refuse them everything, after all, and then I had to watch my step if I didn't want the director sending me off to the special re-education centre. The director said it was a pity that even the best salesgirls went bad, and that you couldn't depend on anything these days. He said that I'd turned into – excuse me – a *real bitch*: those were his very words. Honoré was thrilled. His theories had been confirmed.

Work had corrupted me: now I was moaning when we did it. Soon he wouldn't have anything to do with me, saying that I disgusted him. It was a problem for me, since now I was always the one who wanted it and I had to seek satisfaction at the boutique. Honoré was driving me into debauchery. And I also wonder today to what extent Honoré might have vaguely noticed some changes in my body. Perhaps he was repulsed by my rolls of fat and my complexion, which grew pinker and pinker and sort of freckled with gray spots. It wasn't practical for me to concentrate my sexual activity solely on the boutique, because besides not always finding customers amenable to my new ways, I had to remember to pretend the way I always had before with our long-time patrons. I'll try to express myself as clearly as possible, because I know it's not easy to understand, especially for men. With the new customers, particularly those who let themselves be conveniently tied up, I could now work in my own way, letting myself go, crying out if I felt like it. But with the habitués, even though I had to restrain my ardour and put up with their unnatural fancies (you know what I mean), I sometimes got off anyway. And some of those old customers pointed out to me somewhat reproachfully that my way of shouting had changed considerably. Naturally, since I'd been faking it before. If you follow me. So I had to remember to yell exactly the way I used to. I also had to remember which clients liked me to call out and which didn't. Well, it's hard to pretend when you're feeling real sensations. I don't know if I'm making any sense. I can imagine how shocking and disagreeable it must be to read this sort of thing from a young girl, but I must add that I'm not quite the same, now, as I was before, and that these kinds of considerations are beginning to escape me. In any case, life was growing complicated. In addition to having to disguise my feelings, I grew more and more afraid of my oldest customers, of the outraged phone calls they might make to the director. I no longer enjoyed the director's trust at all and feared I might be fired. Fortunately a wealthy African marabout rented my services for a week at an exorbitant price. The director was delighted with the arrival of this rich Muslim holy man, but he didn't want anything to happen on the premises, as blacks are a delicate matter. The boutique remained closed the entire time and our more excitable patrons simmered down. Many of our habitués, moreover, turned to a so-called treasure that the director had unearthed in the Antilles and installed right on the Champs-Elysées, which makes you wonder where the chain had found the funds. The marabout was charming with me. He took me to his loft in the African quarter and told me he'd been looking for someone like me for a long time. At first we had some fun – he quite appreciated my personality. As for me, I might as well tell you, I learned a thing or two. It's not every day you discover new sensations, particularly as the marabout was an expert in his national specialities. And then, after he'd thoroughly amused himself, he began to do funny things. He rubbed ointments on me and examined me by auscultation, as it were, as though he were looking for something. My skin reacted violently to the ointments, burning, changing colour, and I almost told him to stop. He had me drink a liqueur made from pelicans' eyes. He also tried to hypnotize me. He asked me if I felt ill. To get him to leave me alone for a while, I began to tell him everything that had happened over the past months. The marabout gave me his card and told me to come back and see him *if it continued*. We got on well together. The marabout laughed a lot over the difference in our colours, with him so black and me so pink now, it fired up his appetite. We always had to get down on all fours in front of the mirror and make animal noises. Men are really strange. It's still too soon for me to tell you what I saw in the mirror, you wouldn't believe me. It was so chilling, by the way, that I refused to think about it for a long time. The marabout sent me home at the end of the week. Standing in his doorway, he insisted that I come back to see him *if it got worse*. And he pinched me one last time under my sweater. I thought he did it simply to be nice, the way he gave me twenty extra euros so I could go home in a taxi. But in the stairway I noticed that he'd left a bruise, which took a dramatic turn, you might say. It developed violet and brown accents. Honoré was furious about this week-long training course, and definitely suspicious. I hid the bruise as best I could. Honoré refused to touch me any more, but he hadn't lost the habit of ogling me every evening while I showered, and I also had to submit to a few of his caprices, but only with my mouth. Naked and busy with Honoré like that, I found it hard to hide the bruise, which was just above my right breast. Honoré didn't seem to notice anything, though, and he didn't mention the weight I'd so obviously gained, either. The bruise became a perfectly round circle, pinkish brown. I was a little less eager to have sex – that was passing. The bondage clients bored me. I found the violent ones more and more exhausting. There were some sort of fundamentalists who came as a group to *chastise* me, they said, and the words *wretched girl* were on every tongue. The clientele the director was sending to my boutique kept getting weirder. Even the guy who had chained himself to the operating table at my abortion turned up, and did he ever put me through the mill. Now I was all covered with bruises, but only the one on my chest wouldn't fade away, and it sickened me. It was slowly turning into a teat. Gradually it became sort of nubby, like the skin on nipples, and on the surface appeared a rather distinct lump that even began to show a point. Dealing with all those loonies made me wonder if I wasn't being punished by God, I ask you. Anyway, my periods returned, and that was something, at least. Nothing interested me any more, and my work became very difficult for me. I even began dreaming about a nice quiet little cosmetics shop in a distant suburb where I would simply demonstrate products. I'd fallen quite low. And so had my morale. It was that extra teat that was worrying me, plus my periods, too, strangely enough. I was truly glad to see them come back, but as always they just wiped me out. I was exhausted and no longer had the heart for anything. It's hormonal, apparently. Perhaps I was also a little worried at not having ended up pregnant, seeing as they'd warned me so thoroughly about this at the clinic. My period was exceptionally heavy, a real tidal wave, enough to make you think it was another miscarriage. But I'd decided never to go to another gynaecologist. Besides, I had no money. I understand now that even if I had been pregnant, it could only have ended in a spontaneous abortion. And it was better that way.

I found it hard to get used to my body's new rhythm. I

got my period about every four months, following a short phase of *sexual excitement*, not to mince words. The problem was that although my new clientele was now firmly established, there were still a few of the earlier customers left. I was obliged on the one hand to act as if I were always in heat, on the other to simulate a constant coldness. It was tiring. I was losing track, confusing the times when I was supposed to be faking or hiding something. It wasn't a life any more. I could never be *in tune* with my body, yet the constant refrain of *Gilda Mag* and *My Beauty, My Health*, magazines I received at the boutique, was that if you didn't achieve this harmony with yourself, you risked getting cancer, an *anarchic growth of cells*. I was fleeing ever more frequently to the little park when I was between clients, making them cool their heels. I was risking trouble with the director, but I simply couldn't take it any more. I swiped the products recommended by the magazines and smoothed creams carefully onto my skin, but nothing helped. I was just as fatigued, my head was still in a muddle, and the *special micro-cellular anti-cellulite gel for sensitive skin* from Yerling didn't seem to want to penetrate. Honoré said that it was about the only thing that didn't. Honoré was getting crude, he really suspected something. Besides developing a thick layer of subcutaneous fat, my skin was becoming allergic to everything, even the most expensive preparations. It was thickening disgracefully and became hypersensitive, which was delightful when I was *in heat*, to put it baldly, but a real handicap when it came to makeup, perfumes, and household products, things I obviously had to use at work or when taking care of Honoré's apartment. So it never failed: I'd be covered with scaly red patches that left my skin rosier than ever when they healed. And I rubbed every cream in the world on my third nipple, but nothing helped; it wouldn't go away. When I noticed something like an actual breast swelling beneath it, I thought I was going to faint. If that kept up, I'd have to go to the clinic for an operation, and I was flat broke. The women's mags published the addresses of plastic surgeons, hinting that they'd be more accommodating for obliging cases, but I didn't want to get caught up again in some endless runaround. I desperately needed to relax. I no longer accepted any weekend invitations. Not that I wasn't tempted by those huge country houses any more, but as they say, once bitten, twice shy. A barn, even a stable, would have suited me fine, but on my own, alone. I was still grunting in my sleep; once, I must admit, I wet the bed. I could see Honoré was making an effort not to throw me out. I'm still grateful to him for his kindness, his patience; he had no reason to keep me, since he no longer found me sexually attractive. I even phoned my mother to find out if I could move back in with her in an emergency, but she avoided answering the question. Later I learned that my mother had won a small sum at Lotto and intended to move to the country, but she never mentioned this because she didn't want me sponging off her. My days were now spent trying to find the tiniest minute in which I could slip away between clients. The director had taken me to task for a certain slovenliness, but he didn't realize that my old uniform, which he'd decided not to replace, was nowhere near as sexy as it had been. It was much too tight, the white material had yellowed, and my spare tyre had popped too many seams. I probably looked pathetic. I was so tired. My hair was sticking up like bristles, falling out in handfuls, and I couldn't do a thing with it. I used lotions and set my hair, trying to hide the damage, but my lack of flair for this sort of thing became painfully obvious. I was constantly plagued by skin eruptions that were impossible to conceal since I couldn't use either powder or foundation any more, and of course I no longer put on any makeup – no eyeliner, no mascara – because I was allergic to it all. My eyes now seemed smaller to me in the mirror, closer together than before, and without powder my nose took on a slightly piggy look that was a total disaster. The only thing I could still wear was lipstick. The director forced me to lower my prices, and in order not to reduce the firm's earnings I had to cut my percentage. Now I was making only enough to pay for food and public transportation, and the rest went to Honoré for the rent. The clientele had begun to change again, too. Since prices were dropping and I looked less soignée as well as less hard-to-get, the best clients took offence and left. I still haven't told you the worst part. The worst was the hair. It was growing on my legs, even on my back: long, thin hairs, tough and translucent, that no depilatory could remove. I had to use Honoré's razor on the sly, but by the end of the day I was prickly all over. The customers didn't much care for that. Luckily, I had some regulars left, a handful of gentle wackos who always wanted me down on all fours. They sniffed me, licked me, and went about their business while braying or bellowing like rutting stags, stuff like that. The marabout, who went in for that kind of thing, telephoned me a few times, urging me to come see him for a *consultation*, he said specifically. But I was too tired, and afraid of some new special interest. Fortunately, when I went back into heat, I felt my former zest return and rediscovered a deep interest in my work. And a good thing, too, because the director was just waiting for a chance to trip me up. He wasn't happy with me at all any more. He demanded that I lose weight and wear some makeup. He even bought me a new uniform. 'It's your last chance,' he informed me. But with the best will in the world I couldn't have gone back to being the same person I had been. The boutique suffered another drop in prestige; I'd almost fallen into the lowest category. My customers were really sleazy, without any education. The shop smelled like a zoo, but that wasn't what bothered me. No, what was hard to bear, with all that brutality, was that I no longer received any flowers. So you will understand that I loved to escape to the little park whenever I could, even though this was a clear violation of the most elementary rules of my job. In that public square I always found buttercups, a fresh breath of spring, and I chewed them slowly, secretly. They had the rich taste of succulent grasses. I would watch the birds; there were sparrows, pigeons, sometimes starlings, and their touching little songs brought tears to my eyes. A pair of kestrels had a nest just above the boutique, I'd never noticed it before. At times I felt as though I understood everything the birds said. There were cats, too, and dogs; the dogs always barked when they saw me, while the cats gave me funny looks. I had the impression everyone knew I ate flowers. When summer arrived I no longer found as many flowers and fell back on plain grass; in autumn I discovered horse chestnuts. They have a nice flavour, chestnuts. I didn't bother trying to hide any more, except from any clients who might pass by; I'd realized that nobody could care less about what I was up to. The chestnuts were easy to peel, as my nails had grown quite hard and more curved than before. My teeth were strong, too – I'd never have believed it. The chestnut would crack between my molars, squirting out a thick, delectable juice. Two chomps and it was gone, and I had to have another. One day I was given a euro by my elderly customer's friend, the lady in black. She thought I was going hungry. She wasn't wrong, in a sense. I was constantly hungry, I would have eaten anything at all. I'd have eaten peelings, over-ripe fruit, acorns, earthworms. The only thing I still couldn't stomach was ham, which also meant pâté, sausages, and salami – all those handy luncheon meats. Even chicken sandwiches didn't taste as good as they once had. I ate raw potato sandwiches. From a distance, you would definitely have thought it was sliced hard-boiled egg. One day, Honoré bought me some potted minced pork at a fancy delicatessen. He wanted to please me by doing the shopping for once and by preparing a little *charcuterie* party for the two of us at home. Well when I saw the potted pork, I just threw up then and there, in the kitchen. Honoré glared at me in disgust. I'd blown our last chance, in a way. I was a nervous wreck for the rest of the evening. I was shaking, and the entire apartment reeked from my cold sweats. Honoré stormed out, leaving me alone with that potted pork sitting on the table. I was stuck in the kitchen, since I had to go past the table to get to the living room, and I simply couldn't do it. I had a ghastly night. As soon as I nodded off on my stool, images of blood and butchery flooded my mind. I saw Honoré looming over me, opening his mouth as if for a kiss, then biting me savagely in the bacon. I saw my clients pretending to nibble the flowers at my cleavage so that they could sink their teeth into my neck. I saw the director ripping off my uniform and howling with laughter at discovering six teats instead of two breasts. It was that last nightmare that woke me with a start. I ran to vomit in the bathroom, and the smell of the potted pork made the heaves even worse. It was as though my vitals – guts, tripes, bowels – were turning inside out like a glove. I was uncontrollably sick for a few minutes, after which I felt this compulsion to bathe: I washed my entire body, soaping every last little corner, trying to get clean. A most peculiar odour clung to my skin. The hairs were especially repulsive. I dried myself carefully with a nice fresh towel, patted on some talcum powder, and felt somewhat better. Then I shaved my legs and tried to do the same with my back, nicking myself slightly (it's hard to shave your own back). The sight of the blood petrified me. While the blood trickled out I just sat there on my rump, unable to forget those images of slaughter, the blood spurting from the carotid artery, the body jerking convulsively. Yet I'd never actually seen anyone's throat slit. The only person like that I'd known was my former client, the one who'd been murdered and whose friend came to the little park. This friend had told me they'd merely been polishing her off when they cut her throat, they'd already been working on her for a long time, and there was clotted blood everywhere when she was found. I preferred not to think about it. I know that photos were published in a newspaper; a customer had insisted on giving me a copy and had even wanted me to do special things to him while looking at the pictures. I'd refused. He spoke to the director – the first time a customer of mine had ever complained. Fortunately, it was shortly afterwards that they held the ceremony where I was crowned Best Worker. I'd liked my murdered client, but that wasn't really why I'd refused to look at the photos; it was rather that I'd already sensed that I wouldn't be able to bear the sight of all that blood. On the one hand, I was dreaming about blood night after night and had these vague impulses to hack up some plump flesh. On the other hand, flesh was precisely what repelled me the most. At the time I didn't understand these contradictions very well. Now I know that nature abounds in them, that opposites meet constantly in this world, but I'll spare you my modest ruminations. Still, you should

be aware that now I often chew up one of nature's little creatures without the slightest twinge of either pride or disgust. We all need to get our dose of protein. Mice are the easiest – ask any cat – or else earthworms, but they don't pack as much energy. On the night when I'd bloodied my back, I wasn't able to get up for several hours. Oddly enough, I didn't feel cold. Although I was naked on the tile floor, my skin had grown so thick that it kept me warm, so to speak. When I finally managed to move, it seemed to tear something in me, as though exerting my will required terrific effort from both my brain and my body. I tried to stand up and was sur- •
prised to find my body buckling beneath me. I wound up on all fours. It was frightening, because I couldn't move my hips – as though I were paralyzed in the hindquarters, like an old dog. I strained to get up but it was no use, I couldn't do it. I waited for a long time. It was hard to turn my head to look behind me. I felt as if the bathroom were full of cackling former customers, yet I knew perfectly well I was alone. I was scared stiff. Finally, something seemed to give way in my mind and my body: my will sort of concentrated itself in the small of my back, and I managed to lurch to my feet. It was the worst experience of my life. Later on I still had this con- stant ache in my hips, a kind of cramp, and a certain dif- ficulty in standing very straight. I was so upset by all

this that I had to look at myself in the mirror, to recognize myself, in a way. I saw my poor body, saw how damaged it was. There was nothing – almost nothing – left of my former *radiance*. The skin of my back was red, hairy, with strange greyish spots running down my spine. My thighs, once so firm and well proportioned, sagged beneath a mass of cellulite. My rear end was as smooth and fat as a huge pimple. I had cellulite on my belly, too, but a strange kind, both droopy and stringy. And there, in the mirror, was what I dreaded seeing – not what I'd seen in the marabout's mirror, but something equally horrible. The teat over my right breast had turned into a real dug, and there were three other blotches on the front of my body: one above my left breast and two others, perfectly parallel, just below my real nipples. I counted and recounted, there was no mistake: that made six all right, including three fully formed breasts. Day was dawning. I had a sudden impulse. I threw on a coat and went straight to the Quai de la Mégisserie, the old Tannery Row. I waited for the stores to open. I took my time making my selection. I bought a pretty guinea pig with green eyes, a female, as I was a little turned off by the males with their big things. And then I bought a small dog. They cost me a lot of money. Nowadays, there aren't many animals left. Anyway, I didn't have to buy a leash. The little dog began to follow me on his own with an interested air, constantly sniffing along in my wake. As for the guinea pig, she slept in my arms, cute as a bug, looking happy and peaceful. The doggy checked me out carefully, as if looking for something. He took an immediate and fascinated interest in my case. He pointed me out with his nose to every dog he saw on the street, and they all stared at me, wide-eyed. This pissed me off fairly quickly. I was looking for a companion, someone to understand and comfort me, not exhibit me like a circus freak. I wasn't sorry about the dog when Honoré threw it out the window, only about the money I'd spent on it. Honoré had come home dead drunk. He smelled of female, probably from one of his students. He started right in braying about my *menagerie*. I realized that as a couple we were definitely on our last legs. I screamed that if he touched a hair on the head of my piglet, he, Honoré, would be the one who sailed out the window. I didn't go to work that morning. Or rather, yes, I did open the shop furtively, to steal some perfumes and beauty preparations. I know it wasn't right, and ordinarily I never would have done it, but I was feeling somewhat addled. I went all out on Operation Last Chance. I sold the products on the street and went to see a dermatologist. I simply had to be lovely when Honoré came home. The dermatologist exclaimed indignantly when she examined me, saying

45

she'd never seen skin in such condition before. You might say she really knew how to make a body feel better. I explained to her that all I wanted was to be able to wear some makeup that evening, and to smell less awful. The dermatologist told me she wasn't a beautician. She was quite a stylish woman, so I felt even uglier next to her. She wound up injecting me with some kind of serum, explaining that there were diseases around, especially in public squares, what with all those pigeons. Then she asked me suspiciously if I'd had sexual intercourse lately. I didn't dare answer. She rolled her eyes and administered a second dose of serum. It gave me terrific headaches and nausea. The dermatologist asked me not to vomit on her carpet. All this was quite expensive. That evening, though, I was able to wear makeup with only a modest allergic reaction and to shave more closely than usual. I'd also done something extravagant that afternoon: I'd bought a dress that fit me. The saleslady told me it was the only style they had in that size. The dress was pretty, though: ample, it's true, with a high waist and a stand-up collar, but filmy and light – in short, ultra-feminine. When I got home I was stone broke. But I enjoyed a kind of peace, for a moment. I was able to keep a cup of coffee down and rest awhile in an armchair.

When Honoré came home, he told me I smelled nice. I'd

poured Yerling all over myself. Honoré kissed me on the forehead and told me that since I was looking so lovely that evening, he was inviting me to Aqualand in memory of our first meeting. I could have wept with joy. There was a changing room reserved in Honoré's name when we arrived, which made me feel wonderful. I thought it was a good omen that he'd arranged everything beforehand. In the cubicle Honoré managed to rise to the occasion and sodomize me. I think he couldn't bear even to think about my vagina any more. As for me, bending forward, I had what you might call an unparalleled view of my vulva, and I thought it was dangling rather strangely. I don't want to burden you with details, but the greater labia were hanging down a mite lower than normal, which is why I could see them so well. In *Woman's World* or *My Beauty, My Health*, I don't remember exactly, I'd read that the ancient Romans' favourite – and choicest – dish was stuffed sow's vulva. The magazine had railed against a culinary practice that was both macho and cruel to animals. I took no sides on the subject, never having had any particularly firm opinions on politics. Honoré finished. We left the cubicle. I'd made a point of putting my dress back on for dinner. It would have been a shame not to enjoy such a pretty dress a little more, a dress that fit me, in which I could actually breathe. We had a very pleasant meal. There was a wide selection of exotic salads. Honoré let me eat whatever I wanted, even though it was incredibly expensive. The only thing that bothered me a bit was that I'd left my guinea pig at home, and I missed her already. Luckily Honoré was so charming that he took my mind off her. She was truly a sweet little animal. I thought I was going to be sick when Honoré insisted that I taste his peccary *à l'ananas*, but I managed to control myself. I was quite hot and could feel my makeup running. I hadn't detected the itchy beginnings of any allergic rash yet, fortunately. Beneath the palms, in the imitation trade winds from the fans, you would almost have thought yourself in a tropical paradise. Everything was going splendidly. It was all putting Honoré in top form – which was rather convenient because I could feel myself going into heat again. Honoré stood up before the dessert and told me to join him in the changing room. I was a trifle embarrassed because of those black guys in loincloths who were fanning us, but they'd obviously seen it all before. In the dressing room, Honoré gave me a gift-wrapped package bearing the well-known logo of Moonlight Madness, with the big bow of silvery velveteen ribbon and everything. I began to cry. Honoré scolded me for being so sentimental. In the box was a gorgeous bathing suit, cut very low. Honoré undressed me himself. When he wadded my dress up and tossed it into a corner, I felt

kind of bad to see him treat it so carelessly. Then he had
me put on the bathing suit. I didn't want to, but how
could I refuse? It ripped immediately. Honoré was so
angry he forced me out of the changing room dressed
like that. The black guys didn't even blink, bless them.
Honoré pushed me into the water. The wave machine
was on high. When I hit the water I felt something like a
ripple of terror go through me. I realized that I was
barely staying afloat, and that I hardly knew how to
swim any more. I had to thrash my arms and legs
around directly beneath me, as though my joints were
once again locked into a right angle. I couldn't believe
that I – who had once loved water so much and used to
find such glorious comfort there, in Aqualand, in all that
warm and liquid blue – was now choking, panicking,
struggling in vain, with a wildly pounding heart, to get
out of the pool. Honoré was staggered. He couldn't
deny the facts. I had changed completely from when
we'd first met. A boy reached out to me and I grabbed
his hand, but the little creep let go with a shriek of laughter, calling me a fat cow. I began to cry. Honoré left without looking back, probably dying of shame. When he
returned he had one of those black girls in G strings
from the reception desk on his arm. Everybody knows
about the black receptionists at Aqualand. Honoré stank
of palm wine. Me, I was glad to see him anyway, because

he was the one who had the key to the dressing room where all my things were. I'd hidden as well as I could under a pink vinyl mangrove tree, but I was being bothered by a whole bunch of boys led by the one who'd insulted me. They were pulling at the last strap on my bathing suit, trying to get me to let go of the raggedy scraps still covering my bottom. They were having a ball dancing around me, I'm telling you. Honoré didn't seem too pleased. He sent the receptionist away, so no one would see, I guess, and told me that I'd fooled him but good, that I was absolutely the pits and a disgusting whore. That's what he said. Honoré was weeping. I'd have given anything to console him – it tore at my heart to see him like that. But I couldn't leave my mangrove tree, it would have been indecent. That slutty black woman came back looking for Honoré and I'm no fool, she must have consoled him really well. The last thing Honoré did when he left was to tell the kids to teach me a lesson, so they threw me into the water. There were a good half dozen of them. I almost drowned, and my bathing suit gave up the ghost. When they'd had enough of me I begged them to bring me my dress, or at least a towel, but you can imagine, kids these days are just heartless. They left me in the water. I was exhausted. Aqualand was closing and there I still was, completely naked like an idiot. One of the big black guys supervising the pool came over and told me that if I continued to cause an uproar, he'd call the police, but I knew that with everything going on at Aqualand, he wasn't about to do that. I pleaded with him to bring me something to wear. He started laughing like the stuffed whale that decorates the far end of the room. After a moment, though, he tossed me a kind of bathrobe, but it was way too small. I got out of the water as best I could. Then I saw the police arrive and I thought it was the end, that I, who had always led an honest life, was actually going to be hauled off to jail. I began to sob. But the police weren't there to arrest me. They were accompanying a whole lot of distinguished-looking gentlemen now gathering at the edge of the pool, even though Aqualand had closed. The black women in G strings were placing garlands of flowers around the gentlemen's necks, while the gentlemen were slipping banknotes into their G strings. Couples paired off immediately, guests with black girls, and guests with black guys, too, you do see such things. There were even some who didn't wait any longer before getting down to business, jumping fully clothed into the water with their black guy or girl, which left me speechless. I mean, I did know that the private parties at Aqualand weren't dull, but still, in the water and all. Then someone spoke into a microphone, and a big table laden with refreshments slid out all by itself to the edge of the pool. The gentlemen swarmed over it and some opened champagne bottles in the water, spraying bubbly everywhere, and it's so expensive. A girl on in-line skates came and did a striptease on the catwalk over the water. I was frightened of being discovered, especially since these gentlemen were getting seriously tanked, and I knew from Honoré that alcohol completely perverts people. A man who's been drinking – and I'm speaking here to any girls who will be allowed to read this account – forgets his natural kindness. What is doubtless best for the girls of today, and I venture this opinion on the strength of my extensive experience, is to find a good husband, a teetotaller, because life is hard and a woman doesn't work like a man, and you can't expect men to look after the children, and there aren't enough children, every government says so. The in-line skater finished her number by climbing naked up a palm tree to unroll a huge poster, which made everyone applaud. It said: *Edgar somebody-or-other, for a healthier world*. I tried to listen to the speech that followed, but I've always had trouble concentrating on such stuff, because I didn't have much education. What I did grasp was that the gentleman said things would get better, that we were in a very nasty period of change, but that he'd pull us through. I learned that there were going to be elections. Edgar seemed nice, I thought I'd be safe enough after all, and that if the situation turned sour I could always promise to vote for him. I emerged as discreetly as possible from the shelter of my mangrove. Everyone was drunk. There was deafening music now, the lights went out, and I thought that this would help me make my escape. Some laser beams or whatever started whirling all around the room; people were jumping up and down and pushing one another into the water, which slowed me down somewhat. I stumbled right into the clutches of a guy who was cold sober. He held a big revolver up to my temple. I thought I was going to die. He shoved me into a small room off to the side. Some gentlemen in bulletproof vests asked me loads of questions. I told them I'd come to have dinner with Honoré, and he'd given me a bathing suit, and my suit had fallen apart, but this didn't seem to satisfy them. The one with the biggest revolver spoke into a portable phone, asking what they should do with me. He looked at me and said, 'No, not so hot.' That hurt. Then he hung up, and turning to his men he added, 'The bosses never leave us anything but the pigs.' That hurt even more. But the men looked at me as if they were the ones who'd been insulted. I was really scared. In the end they didn't kill me. They merely fooled around a bit with their dogs. And then they looked sort of grossed out and stopped us just at the best moment. One of the men pulled out his revolver and said, 'The bitch should be shot.' I hadn't seen anything but males. It's only now that I get what he meant. That's when a gentleman in a suit walked in. He asked what was going on there and, rather gallantly, helped me to my feet. The men in bulletproof vests said nothing and the guy who'd been all steamed up put his gun away. The gentleman said he'd heard cries, like the squeals of a pig having its throat cut. He looked at me with a kind of pity. He took me away and offered me a glass of rum. You could tell he was thinking about something as he watched me. He asked me how I felt and everything. Then he tossed me a towel so I could clean myself up and he sent one of the receptionists to get me a dress. Imagine that, two new dresses in one day. And pretty ones, too. The gentleman called someone on his portable phone and then – you won't believe this – one of my former co-workers in the boutique showed up. She didn't say anything but it was eye-poppingly obvious that she was wondering what anyone would see in me and why she wasn't there instead of me. She pulled a lot when she did my hair, saying she just couldn't do anything with it, but the gentleman said it didn't matter. 'The more she looks like a hayseed, the better,' he said. I didn't dare protest. The salesgirl made me up. She rather accentuated the farm-girlish red of my cheeks. I could tell she was doing it on purpose, I knew my way around makeup by then. I had only one fear: that the effect of the dermatologist's serum would wear off too soon. Wrinkling up her nose, the salesgirl sprinkled Moonlight Madness perfume on me. The gentleman sent her away and had me come with him to an office where I saw Monsieur Edgar, two other nattily attired gentlemen, and a couple of girls. 'I found a real pearl,' he announced triumphantly. Then Edgar and the two other men gazed at me in ecstasy. It sure helped my morale, I can tell you. They pinched me everywhere, checked my teeth and the whites of my eyes, made me turn around, smile, and then they sent the other girls away. I was already dreaming of a big career in the movies, and you know, I wasn't far wrong. Picture this: two minutes later a photographer with a Polaroid zeroed in on me. Then the gentlemen ignored me completely as they all pored over the photos while I waited around, wondering what it was they wanted from me. 'For a healthier world!' one of them began to bellow, and they all guffawed. I thought they were making fun of me. The photographer took me home. I had to pose for his photos all night long, and just a minute while I change the lighting, and hang on while I repowder your snout. Well, the dermatologist's serum was hanging on, but I was wiped out. After the emotion and all, I felt I'd had enough for one day. I was yawning and the photographer was cursing me. I had to smile, and pose like this and that, I mean really. The photographer sent me off with a wad of bills in my hand. I thought that was fair. The one thing I regretted was not having seen the end of the party at Aqualand, when I'd never in my whole life been invited to such a high-class affair.

I went back to Honoré's apartment because I didn't know where else to go. I had an unpleasant surprise. Honoré had put all my things out on the landing: my cosmetics samples, my underwear, my too-tight white smock and grey pants. It was lucky for me that I'd left Aqualand with a wearable dress. I gathered all my stuff together. When I picked up my uniform, I noticed it was bloodstained. I dropped it immediately, in disgust. It plopped softly when it hit the floor. Honoré had cut my little guinea pig's throat and put the body in the front pocket of my smock. I couldn't touch that uniform again. I was sick to my stomach. Vomit and pig's blood were all over the landing. Honoré wasn't going to be happy when he opened the door. As I left I had trouble walking. My hips were aching badly and my head felt so heavy that I kept falling forward. It was hard to keep my neck straight. The strain cramped the muscles of my shoulders and lower back. I set out, trudging through the suburb. Dawn was breaking. In a dustbin I found

two plastic bags for my belongings – they were easier to
carry that way. My joints hurt so much I had to rest on a
bench. It felt good to slump there for a while. Birds
began to sing. I recognized the blackbirds, and there was
even a nightingale over by the smokestacks of Issy-les-
Moulineaux. I hadn't known until that moment that I
could recognize the song of a nightingale. There were
also a few rats looking for something to eat around the
edges of the sewer gratings, and some tiny yellow mice,
and a cat lying in wait for prey. I watched the cat's little
tricks for a long time. It made me hungry. The previous
evening I'd had only tropical salad to eat, and besides
I'd thrown it all up. The sky was a pale grey streaked
with pink, and the smoke from the factories was bright
green against the sunrise. I don't know why this had
such an effect on me. I guess I was truly moved. The
blackbirds and the nightingale began to quiet down, and
then it was the sparrows chirping, the nestlings clam-
ouring for their rations. I felt unbelievably awake and
famished. I rolled onto my side and off the bench. I
landed on all fours. I was standing firmly on the ground,
which felt solid beneath me, and I no longer hurt anywhere, as though my body were thoroughly rested.
Then I began to eat. There were acorns and horse chestnuts. In that area of the suburb they'd planted American
oaks that turn a brilliant red in autumn. The acorns were

especially delicious, with something like a faint flavour of virgin soil. They cracked between the teeth, the fibres softened in the saliva – it was hearty, crunchy fare, quite satisfying. I had a strong taste of earth and water in my mouth, the taste of forest, of dead leaves. There were lots of roots, too, smelling nicely of liquorice, witch hazel, gentian, and they slipped down my throat like a sweet dessert, festooning me with long strands of sugary drool. Belching gently, I stuck out my tongue and licked my chops. I saw the shadow of someone passing by and managed to straighten up a little, pretending that I was looking for something. The shadow vanished. But others appeared on the street corner. Gritting my teeth, I sat down on the bench. I found a paper napkin in a rubbish basket and wiped my face, which was covered with spittle and smears of dirt. I wasn't hungry any more, I'd eaten enough. I sat there for a good long time. Birds landed on me and pecked at my cheeks, the corners of my mouth, behind my ears, where scraps of food remained. That tickled me, and I laughed in great flutterings of wings. More and more shadows passed by. The sun was almost up; the sky was grey and gold. People were going off to the Métro. No one looked at me, yet they were passing right in front of the bench, walking around my plastic bags. They all seemed weary. There were also a few women with babies in pushchairs:

fat, pink babies. I almost longed to place them at my breast, or to nudge them with my nose, playing, biting. The sky was brightening overhead. From where I was sitting, I could see lights twinkling high in the tower where Honoré lived. I couldn't tell exactly which was his window, but I pictured him badly shaven, hung over, perhaps with the black girl still there to make him coffee. It's sad to say, but I was better off where I was. Only, the black girl probably wouldn't know how to fix him just what he needed to get him back on his feet after a binge. You really had to be Honoré's girl, someone who knew how to take care of him. It would certainly have been simpler if I'd agreed to stay home, have a baby, and all that. I had regrets, and I was also ashamed of having failed, yet at the same time I wanted to see the end of the sunrise. I know it's hard to understand, but I didn't feel at all like working any more. I had a pocket full of money, which wasn't going to last for ever and of course I really should have put it aside, but I also told myself that once I'd bought a new uniform to go back to work, I wouldn't have much left. And then the pigeons started their cooing. There was an extremely myopic little bat, too, that hadn't managed to find its way home and was flitting back and forth, stuffed with gnats. I could clearly hear the quavering distress in its blindly uttered ultra-sonic cries, its fear at the prospect of being caught out in daylight. There wasn't much I could do for it. I missed my guinea pig. The sun, curiously enough, was taking for ever to rise. Over by Issy, it was growing harder to make out the factory smoke, the colours were running together. All I could see now was the vivid red background of the sky, while everything else was light and dark shadows. I rubbed my eyes. My normal vision returned. I even thought I spied Honoré's lights go out. A few minutes later he passed in front of me, on his way to take the Métro and then the bus to work. For the next two or three days I stayed on the bench to see Honoré go by. Then Sunday must have come, because he didn't. I was hesitant about going to Mass. I had a strange feeling of both wellbeing and uneasiness, I don't know how to put it; I thought that going to Communion might be good for me. It was getting harder for me to walk, too, and since I wasn't spending any of my money, while eating and sleeping under the oak trees, I figured I might do well to consult a doctor. I was becoming convinced there was something in my brain, a tumour, I don't know what, something that might be paralyzing my hindquarters, disturbing my vision, and upsetting my digestion. I no longer even tried to eat anything I hadn't found on the ground, it wasn't worth it, I simply threw up. I carefully avoided thinking about meat, about everything that might resemble sausage, blood, ham, offal. What made me decide to go to Mass was that they cut down the oaks to erect a billboard. The workmen didn't pay much attention to me, they merely moved my bench out of their way. A chainsaw does a quick job. The freshly cut wood smelled nice, but I felt rather sorry to see the trees bracing themselves with all their strength only to collapse, moaning. Where was I going to live now? I nibbled a few shavings. A workman gave me part of his sandwich, saying, 'It's really a shame.' Well, I tried to thank him but couldn't speak clearly! So much for going to confession, I thought. It was a ham sandwich. I let go of it, it fell in the dirt, and the workman didn't look too pleased. So I got up from the bench, which wasn't easy, and that's when I saw the photo they'd put up on the brand-new billboard. It was me. What I mean is, at first I thought that the person reminded me of someone. A workman was giving me a funny look. That helped me along. He'd recognized me, or rather I think he'd recognized the dress, which looked great in the picture, better than on me, anyway, because it was already covered with dirt stains and acorn juice. It began to rain. This made my vision a bit blurry but I believe I was crying as well. The dress was very lovely, red with scallops and a white apron, and I did have some trouble recognizing myself, but there could be no mistake about the look in her eyes. Which is to say, what

I thought I saw at first was a pig wearing that beautiful red dress, a kind of female pig – a sow, if you like – and in her eyes was that hangdog look I get when I'm tired. You can understand, though, that it was hard for me to see myself in her. Then I decided that it was only an optical illusion, that the intense red colour of the dress was giving me that deep pink complexion in the photo, making me seem much rosier than I really was despite my chronic allergies, and I thought I could see how the impression of a snout, slightly protuberant ears, teeny eyes, and so on was simply caused by the rustic atmosphere of the poster, and especially by those extra pounds I'd put on. Take a perfectly healthy girl, put her in a red dress, have her gain a smidgen of weight, tire her out, and you'll see what I mean. Once I'd realized how the illusion worked, I did in fact recognize myself in the poster. And then I resolved sincerely to slim down, and to pull myself together. That photo helped me to stand up. That photo helped me to understand that I had to bathe, to leave that bench, to get a grip on things again. I felt worn out just thinking about it but I had to do it. So you could say I owe Edgar more than I can ever repay. I decided to go to Mass. In front of the church it dawned on me that I was getting kind of dumb, because Mass is on Sunday, of course, and I'd just seen some workmen on the job. So it had to be Monday or Tuesday, perhaps

Wednesday. I'd missed seeing Honoré go by, or else I hadn't recognized him. I realized that I no longer remembered Honoré's face very well: no matter how hard I concentrated, his image eluded my memory. The church was open. I went inside. I made the sign of the cross over the holy-water basin, and kneeling down, I tried to pray. Would you believe it, I couldn't recall what came after 'Hallowed be Thy name'! I must have seemed so bewildered that a priest came over and asked me what I was doing there. I told him I wanted to make confession. We went into that box-thing. I don't know why, I felt uncomfortable in that church. In the wrong place, basically. I'd left my plastic bags at the entrance, where they looked sort of shabby, I admit. The high vault and so forth were fine, but my spirit wasn't getting the desired uplift. Maybe it was the presence of this priest. I heard him sniffling on the other side of the grating; they'd installed those plastic windows, fortunately, or I'd have been afraid of catching his germs. The priest asked me if I was ill. I said I wasn't ill but I felt weird. The priest told me to pray and repent. I repented as hard as I could. It had been quite a while since my last confession – at my First Communion, actually – but the whole business had made a big impression on me and at the time I'd felt that eating Christ's body had done me a world of good. I wanted to eat it again. But the priest didn't want to give me any. He said that I hadn't told him everything. He told me that there were lots of diseases going around and that they afflicted only those who had sinned and that anyone could tell from my face that I was sick. Through the hygienic window I could see he was holding a handkerchief to his nose. The priest's face was all distorted by the two sheets of plastic, which gave him popping eyes, a dog's muzzle, and these bizarre wrinkles, as if you were seeing double. The priest was studying me, you might say. I didn't know what else I could tell him. I tried to concentrate, but it was no use, there was something about the way the priest was looking at me, and then the smell of his black cassock, and of his skin, too. That stale, insipid odour reached me with unusual intensity, along with the odours of incense and saltpetre, the smell of dried-out palm fronds, and the mustiness of the old pictures hanging on the walls. It was cold and damp in that church, and very dark; I was having more and more trouble seeing the priest and I wanted to sneeze, to curl up on my seat and go to sleep. 'Leave!' the priest told me. I paid him through the little opening and left. My bags had been stolen, but I didn't care. I felt better outside. I didn't want to go see a doctor right away, I'd had enough rehabilitation for one day. I was so tired. I went back to my bench and slept huddled up on it. It was still raining.

When I awoke I saw through a break in the clouds that the sun was halfway home; there was a smell of evening in the air. I was ashamed. This was hardly the way to spruce myself up, getting soaking wet from sleeping on my bench all the time. And now that I'd lost my job at Perfumes Plus, I'd certainly have to find another when my money ran out. I got up and walked as much as I could. I had shooting pains in my neck, my hips, and the small of my back. I often had to stop and flex my shoulders to relieve the tension in my spine. Gradually I began to walk hunched over. I could see myself in the store windows: I looked pretty peculiar. I arrived at the boutique, not quite sure what I was doing there. Sniffing the breeze, I picked up the odour of a sweating woman scented with Yerling, and the characteristic smell of busy days: massage oil and cold sperm. I sat on a bench in the little park. The lady in black was there but she didn't seem to recognize me. I tucked my legs beneath me to ease my back pain and hunched my shoulders. I felt my breasts hanging down, heavy and painful, a burden to lug around, which is perhaps why my back hurt so much when I walked. You could see the shop window from the bench. For the moment the place looked empty; the lined silk curtains had been closed. They must have been giving a massage in the back room, in the lovely salon full of gilt sofas, deluxe gris-gris for potency, and burners for aphrodisiac incense. I felt as though I were right there: I could see everything clearly just by staring at the curtain, as if I were looking straight through it. Given the director's high standards, it must have been difficult to select my replacement for this demanding position. The only thing I regretted was not having trained to become a *chiromancer*, I think that's the word. You see, I'd taken the manicuring class in the evening and all, but the *ne plus ultra* was to know how to read palms. Since I hadn't had much education, the director had promised to have me get that diploma at least, at the City Centre University, where he had connections. Salesgirls with diplomas would have brought increased prestige to his firm. That was one good thing about the business, at any rate, sound professional training, and when I think about it, it wasn't a bad career. It saddened me to think that now I would remain a poor dumb creature. I wondered what would become of me, but the wad of bills in my pocket reassured me. I told myself that I had time to think about it and that after all I'd managed to amount to something in life. A light came on behind the curtain and I picked up the scent of the shopgirl who had given me a so-called hairdo at Aqualand. In addition to earning extra money over there, that bitch had been promoted within the firm and stolen my job. It pained me to see how beautiful she was

and how enthusiastically the client was reaming her
butt. I could see in spite of the curtain – I had a kind of
strange sixth sense, whole new eyes. The client was a
former customer of mine, one of those very old, very
rich, very depraved clients who paid quite a lot of
money for the deluxe ointments, dildoes, and fetishes. I
could tell it was he behind the curtain, he and no one
else, one of the shop's best customers – I was picking up
a kind of shimmering in the air around him, and a
crumbly, papery smell. Well, if that was the kind of customer the salesgirl liked, she could have him. And then
I sensed a familiar presence coming down the street: the
marabout was heading towards the boutique. He'd been
supplying African products to the chain for a while now
and had learned how to dress unobtrusively around
their elegant clientele, abandoning his awful native cos-
tumes. In exchange the director gave the marabout dis-
counts on the Moonlight Madness ultra-whitening
creams for black skin and on all the services offered by
the salesgirls of Perfumes Plus. I saw he was taking
advantage of this, the pig, which rather pained me when
I recalled the wonderful week we'd spent together. I
couldn't imagine what the marabout saw in that slutty
salesgirl, who stank a mile away – like redheads always
do – and in spite of all the fancy fragrance in the world.
The marabout claimed to be a medium, yet he passed by

without seeing me. I was disappointed in him. But to my amazement, the marabout didn't enter the shop. He sat down next to the lady in black. They talked for a long time, then left together. The little square was empty. All of a sudden I felt extraordinarily alone. I heard a familiar grating noise, just barely perceptible. It was the electric shutter coming down. I smelled the scent of sweat and Yerling swirling in the street. The sun was setting. I was having great trouble seeing again, as though I'd become myopic, like the pipistrelles. These small bats were waking up around me. They made a tremendous din. I heard sparrows in the treetops, ruffling their feathers as they went early to bed, batting their eyelids silkily in a final reflex before sleep, and I felt their dreams glide across my skin with the last rays of the sunset. The dreams of birds were everywhere in the warm shadows of the trees, and the dreams of pipistrelles were everywhere in the sky, because pipistrelles dream even when awake. They were so moving, all these dreams. A dog trotted towards me to pee and I sensed that he wanted to talk to me, so to speak, and then he changed his mind and prudently rejoined his master. In the core of my being, I felt a violent, terrifying, delicious sense of solitude – all in the same moment. I don't know if you can understand what I mean. There was no longer anything to keep me in the city, among people. If I hadn't been so heavy, I could have flown away like the birds. But my rump, my breasts, all that flesh went with me everywhere. Not only did my spine ache, my chest hurt, too. I didn't want to lift up my dress to check on my spots, and my new breast pulled painfully beneath the skin, the way they do at puberty. I bent forward, and all that suffering disappeared. My dress stuck out stiffly around me, smelling richly of fresh sweat, warm crotch, living flesh. I curled up in my smell to keep myself company. The birds fell silent. I slipped off the bench and slept there, on the ground, until dawn. In my dreams were the dreams of the birds, and the dream the dog had left for me. I was no longer so alone. I didn't dream about blood any more. I dreamed of ferns and damp earth. My body kept me warm. I was just fine. When the sun came up I felt the light run along my back and turn bright yellow in my head. I got up on my trotters. I shook my head and stretched my hams. My two hands were planted in the soil. They had only three fingers now. I shifted all my weight to the left hand and was able to free the right one. I shook the dirt off it, then I shook my whole body. My hand had five fingers again. I hadn't got a good look at it, but suddenly I was frightened. I remembered what I hadn't wanted to see in the marabout's mirror: the little corkscrew tail on my rear end. I began trembling. My hand was almost numb, curled in, and I couldn't open it all the way. I shook my left hand and saw that the little finger, the *auricular finger*, as it's called, was now shorter. The nail was long and hard, quite thick, as were all the other nails. I hadn't trimmed them in quite a while, I must say, but you would almost have thought that the finger was missing a joint, or at least that the fingertip had atrophied into some tough, horny material. So there was no point any more in wishing I'd taken that palmistry class. I took a deep breath and stood up straight, which almost made me gasp. The sun was climbing in the sky. My dress was all torn from the bushes, so I must have wallowed about a lot in my sleep.

I longed to take a shower somewhere. I'd lost the key to Honoré's apartment with my bags at the church. As for the little bathroom at Perfumes Plus, with the jacuzzi and aromatic oils, I risked finding it occupied even at dawn, because it was often used for various extras. (You could certainly say that the profession also has its drawbacks, like fatigue and overwork.) I had this strange floating feeling. The streets were full of mud because of the previous day's downpours and the *chronic deterioration of the public thoroughfares*. I was hobbling painfully along, trying to avoid the puddles so as not to dirty my poor dress any further, thinking about a possible hotel, not too expensive, perhaps along the ring road. But somehow, I don't know, the mud seemed to be making me dizzy. I went a few hundred yards and sat down on a bench in a tiny square near a car park. There was a rather young woman trying to fold up a pushchair so she could put it in her car boot. A baby was in a car seat sitting on the ground, surrounded by all sorts of stuff: suitcases, baskets, a hamper, toys, packages of nappies. I went over to them. The woman looked exhausted, with a puffy face and red blotches under her eyes. The baby was shrieking. I tried to strike up a conversation but wasn't able to get any words out. It had been days and days since I'd spoken, since I'd found nothing to say to the priest. I opened my mouth but managed to produce only a sort of grunt. The baby gave me a quizzical look and sobbed all the harder. The sight of me seemed to frighten the woman. She slammed down the hood of the boot, half crushing the pushchair, and snatched up the car seat, which almost completely hid her from view. I went up close to the baby. I sniffed at it. It smelled pleasantly of milk and almonds. Oh, perhaps it would have helped me if I could have clung to the woman's legs, heard her speak nicely to me, and perhaps I might have accompanied both of them wherever they were going. I nudged the baby with my nose, the woman began to yell, and as for the baby, I don't know whether it was laughing or crying. I think – how shall I put it – that I could easily have eaten the baby, sunk my teeth into that really rosy flesh, or that I could have carried it off, if the woman had given it to me. The baby smelled so good, and seemed so roly-poly, like an inflatable doll. The woman screamed and ran off with the car seat in her arms. She left everything else on the ground. I started poking around. There was a full baby bottle, which I guzzled in two seconds. It was warm and sweet. I took the big package of clean nappies apart with my snout, and in a basket I found some delectable apples that I enjoyed very much. I ripped open the suitcases but they contained only clothes. I chewed on a few plastic toys to sharpen my teeth, and then I broke some little jars to see if they were tasty. They weren't bad, I got some protein there. I nicked my tongue while I was licking the glass shards and I must have swallowed a few of them, too, because I felt them crunching between my molars. I belched and sat down on the ground. When I looked at the car in front of me and all that abandoned stuff, I had something like a burst of insight: I figured that the woman must have been leaving her home for good, taking her baby and belongings and walking out on who knows what kind of husband. I felt bad at having caused her more trouble. I went over to the car and tried to tidy things up, but that didn't work, so in despair I trampled everything. Spotting a dress sticking out of a suitcase, I pulled it free with my teeth. I thought it might do to replace my dirty one. I dragged the dress over to the bench. I placed it on the seat as carefully as I could. And then, beneath the bench, I spied a puddle. A lovely puddle with nice sun-warmed mud and freshly fallen rainwater. I lay down in the puddle and stretched out my limbs, which eased my joints no end. Then I rolled in it a few times. It was delightful, refreshingly cool on my irritated skin and relaxing for my muscles, like a massage for my back and hips. I half dozed off. I was all perfumed with mud and humus and my nose was pointing downwind, a big mistake. I didn't smell the people coming. Luckily, they stopped when they saw me. I sensed their presence in time and turned around to see the woman, the baby, and a policeman. 'It's monstrous!' exclaimed the policeman. His hand shook as he drew his weapon – which is what saved me. I just had time to snatch up the dress with my teeth and run, run right across the boulevard, dodging honking cars. I hid in a doorway. Afterwards, I had the worst time escaping from this neighbourhood because they'd blocked off the streets and organized a search with dogs. Fortunately, I'd seen some enormous rats come out from under a loose manhole cover, which I shoved aside with my nose. I was able to go underground. I don't know how much time I spent in the sewers. It wasn't so bad there.

It was warm, with mud of a good covering consistency. One night I came back up again. I wanted to go out to the country, where I felt I'd be better off. I was starting to go hungry underground – I'm not a rat, after all. There were election posters all over the walls on the street where I'd come back up. Some of the posters were for my candidate, if I may call him that, who was smiling beside me in an inset photo, and that night, in the gleam of the streetlights, I thought I looked pretty good, pink and blooming. It was the makeup, of course, and the lighting, but it cheered me up to see that I was photogenic in my little dress after all, and that I looked well rounded and healthy. *For a healthier world* was written in big letters between Edgar and me. I thought the slogan *perfect* for the occasion. I mean, I'd just stepped out of a sewer. I hadn't lost all sense of propriety. Okay, I told myself, let's make an effort. In the back of my mind I found that old idea of going to take a shower, and in the bottom of my pocket I found the wad of bills, somewhat damp, but intact. I took a deep breath. I let out a karate shout, and ha! I stood up. The pain in my back was stunning. When I saw my dress, all stretched out over my front and swollen by my six teats, I felt depressed, especially since it still looked so crisp and becoming on the poster. I was in strange shape, I must say. A shower, I kept saying to myself. I walked as fast as I could. I went into a hotel on the ring road. I put a bill into a machine and received a magnetic card that opened the doors to the hotel room and the bathroom right next to it. The hotel seemed empty, but it was because everything was done with these magnetic cards. I undressed in my room, took a nice clean bathrobe from its plastic bag marked *with our compliments*, and went next door to take a shower. I scrubbed hard. At first the water seemed weird to me. Then I drank my fill and decided it was like rain. I shook myself off and rolled on the tiles a little, but they were hard and cold. The soap *with our compliments* made me think of the boutique, as well as of the most delicious roots, because it smelled invitingly of witch hazel. I nibbled one end but this time my snack was revolting. I wondered which I liked better, the roots or the boutique. In any case, the sewers were just too filthy, after all, and most importantly, there wasn't enough light. There were always the crocodiles to watch out for, too. I cried a bit, in the shower, which rather relaxed me. I couldn't figure out what I ought to do next. The hotel was like a kind of airlock between the city and the ring road. Everything there was automatic. From my window I could see people entering and leaving. I was careful to avoid meeting them. They all seemed to know where they were going and what they planned to do, whereas I wasn't doing anything. I was watching television, taking

showers, looking out the window at the smokestacks of
Issy-les-Moulineaux, a few birds in the sky, huge car
parks, supermarkets. I spent several days in that hotel,
lying on my bed between showers. Once a day I'd go
downstairs to put a bill into the machine. I enjoyed looking at myself in the mirror in my room. I was squeaky
clean. I rested. I stayed on my bed and my back didn't
hurt any more. My face was less puffy. I tried to look
human again, sleeping a lot, combing my hair. Almost
all my hair had fallen out in the sewers but it was growing back now. I bit my nails, shaved my legs, and
watched my dugs become less swollen, less visible, until
only the dark spots of the nipples remained. I'd even
washed my dress in preparation for the day when I'd be
leaving. As time went by, I became friendly with the
cleaning man. Lack of exercise had made me much thinner. Using sign language, I arranged with the cleaning
man to have him bring me hamburgers every day. They
were eighty per cent soy and went down easily, along
with ketchup and lettuce. The weight I began to put on
was now more attractively distributed. Eventually I had
no more money to put in the machine, so I got the cleaning man to break the magnetic lock on my room in
exchange for the right to come see me twice a day. He
even showed me how to take free showers by wedging
the door with my outdated card, but I almost drowned –

he hadn't warned me that the stall was automatically disinfected after each use. I wound up with a dandy allergic reaction, but he took care of me kindly. Since he spoke Arabic, conversation wasn't a problem: we didn't speak aloud, we talked by signs, and liked each other fine. Somehow, I was able to get back into my old clothes again after a while. What I mean is, the dress I'd stolen from the woman's suitcase looked all right on me, even fit me at the waist. Perhaps it was the shower, or the burgers, or sleeping in a real bed, or maybe daily contact with the cleaning man. He fell in love with me, the cleaning man. I will admit I was fairly alluring once more, and I myself would have been quite willing to spend the rest of my days in that hotel with him. I decorated my room with flowers I picked along the beltway in the evening, I didn't eat them or anything. The cleaning man did the housekeeping daily, my room was as neat as a pin. One day he gave me a photomat picture of himself and I hung it on the wall. Things were getting cosy. I wound up pregnant, no doubt about it this time. I managed to understand what the cleaning man's name was but not to pronounce it, which means, alas, that I don't remember it now. He made a big fuss over me when he realized I was in an interesting condition. Edgar What's-His-Name won the election. I saw him on TV, posing in front of my poster. He seemed just thrilled. I was happy for him. I was able to compare my face on the TV and my reflection in the mirror: I was completely presentable again. I decided it would be a good idea if I went to find Edgar to ask him for a job. I was sure his party would give me one, since I was their figurehead, their *charismatic leader*, in a way. So as it turned out I'd made some ace connections, I'd bet on the right horse by backing Edgar. I resolved to improve my appearance even more. I gave myself a week to lose additional pounds, stand up perfectly straight, perhaps manage to wear a touch of makeup, and speak clearly. From then on I refused the cleaning man's hamburgers, and he thoroughly disapproved of my eating nothing but salad. My complexion became less ruddy. The first weeks of my pregnancy tired me out and hollowed my cheeks. And then policemen came to the hotel and arrested the cleaning man. I never saw him again, except once on TV: men with machine guns were making him get on a plane with some other people and he was crying. It upset me, but these were the first measures of Edgar's programme. Since the hotel didn't find anyone else to clean the toilets and the beds and all that, the place became fairly squalid. The only things that still worked were the self-disinfecting showers, but they often malfunctioned and drowned a few guests. The hotel was shut down and I found myself back out on the street. I figured that since

Edgar had kicked out all the Arabs, he could easily give me some work. He was the right horse, that Edgar. But I don't know what happened, maybe the shock of finding myself outside, or else the cleaning man's going away – I got wicked cramps smack in the middle of the street. I hunched over and saw that I was losing blood. I fainted. A Mobile Crisis Intervention Unit arrived and they're the ones who revived me. I felt woozy. The policeman with them said, 'You should call the Society for the Protection of Animals instead!' On the ground next to me were six tiny wriggling things covered with blood. Given what they looked like, I could tell they weren't long for this world. The policeman tried to come closer and I bared my teeth. The caseworkers didn't dare lay a hand on me. I struggled to my feet with this terrific pain in my belly. I took the six little things in my mouth, smashed in a manhole cover, and disappeared underground. I licked the poor mites as carefully as I could. When they grew cold, I felt as though I couldn't go on. I curled up in a ball and didn't think about anything any more.

What got me going again was that invasion of piranhas. Everybody cleared out. I wasn't about to stay behind. More and more people now are adopting incredible pets and when they've had enough, plop! Into the sewers.

When I saw the piranhas and felt those first bites, a shiver of fear went right through me, I freaked and raced to get out. I hadn't known that I still cared that much about life. You could say it woke me up. My neurons fell back into place. Outside, in the fresh air, I was able to calm down, organize my thoughts. I managed to stand upright. Now I really had to find some clothes if I wanted to walk around in that city again, and I took up with a group of homeless people. It wasn't easy at first. Me, I had a frank, natural odour – they loved that great country perfume – but as for the smell of unwashed urbanites, I admit I don't much care for it. And then it had been a while since they'd been around a woman, especially one as porky as I was. They took advantage, understandably. Still, they did give me a sort of raincoat and a bite to eat. In the evening, down by the tracks where they slept, the big game was to elude the Mobile Crisis Intervention Units, as the last thing my pals the homeless wanted was to get run in. With me they had everything they wanted, after all, plus I fixed their grub and I wasn't much for talking – the answer to their prayers, you might say. Living with them, I regained a certain dignity. Those of them who'd voted had chosen Edgar and were waiting for him to come see them. I created a sensation when I succeeded in saying that I knew Edgar. I don't know what astonished them more, that I should suddenly speak, or that I knew Edgar. I wanted to prove it to them, so we found a tattered old poster on one of the walls of the train station, but even comparing me with the photo, they couldn't see the resemblance. I could see it just fine, I was distressed that they didn't recognize me. That evening I was treated to a thrashing for having lied. The one time I opened my mouth. I was getting a little fed up with my pals the homeless. To show them, I decided to find Edgar and come back to see them in decent clothes with a nice hairdo and a whole new job. One evening I slipped away and got into one of the Mobile Crisis Intervention vans. There they told me the only public occupations that would be open to women from now on were those of 'personal assistant' or 'travelling companion.' All the cosmetics boutiques were going to be closed down by the vice squad, and I worried about the director of Perfumes Plus. The MCIU caseworkers told me, however, that by knowing the right people I would surely manage to get hired as a wet nurse in the ritzy neighbourhoods, or as a masseuse at the Palace, except you had to be a real knockout for that job, which irritated me, them thinking they had to add that last part. They also said that they themselves, the MCIU, were going to disappear soon, that I was wise to take advantage of them, that they were going to give me hot food and some decent clothing. The driver told me that if I needed to get pregnant to become a wet nurse, he would volunteer his services. That's when I realized all was not lost and that I could still be competitive in my field. But I wasn't able to get pregnant. It must have been the wrong moment in my oestrus cycle, which I hadn't really figured out yet. I stayed at the MCIU centre for several days. The police came to provide me with the proper identification papers in exchange for some background information on my homeless buddies. When I went back down by the tracks to show myself off, all clean and nicely dressed, the tramps had gone, leaving nothing but ashes and bits of charred clothing strewn along the rails. I looked everywhere, but the *clochards* had probably taken off down the tracks the way they'd often talked of doing. Well, looking down the tracks always started me dreaming. I sat down at the edge of the roadbed and tried to think about my future. I decided that if contacting Edgar didn't lead to anything, I'd set out walking along the tracks, because there had to be trees and countryside at the end of the line. That evening at the MCIU centre more and more people kept gathering and shouting really loud; they asked me if I'd hide some weapons under my mattress, saying no one would ever suspect me of anything. I could smell trouble brewing. The police came and permanently closed the MCIU shelter. They didn't find the weapons but they shot people in front of the door and arrested me as an offence to public decency. And my papers were all in order, too! Seeing people die, that did something to me. I began letting out these cries from deep inside me, the way I had when my children died. The police tried to cuff me and I saw their eyes bug out. When I looked at myself in the rearview mirror I realized they were scared of me: I was getting that grotesque pink face back again, with the big snout and long ears. The police wouldn't touch me after that and I wound up in an ambulance. All my hair fell out in the asylum, but I could play with my ears the way I had with my hair, flirtatiously. No one paid any attention to me. I couldn't walk upright at all any more and slept in my own shit; it kept me warm, and I liked the smell. I became chummy with lots of people. No one talked in there, they all screamed, sang, drooled, ate on all fours and that kind of thing. We had fun. There weren't any more *psychiatrists* because the police had carted them all off one day, and some of their bodies were even rotting in the courtyard – shots had been heard. We had a frigging ball in there, I'm telling you, with no one around to bother us. Every once in a while I'd be sort of jolted by this idea, that I should go see Edgar. The problem was that the gates were chained shut, and we'd run out of food. Some of us had begun to be seriously hungry. Me, with my reserves, I was okay, but I saw some others ogling me with that same look I'd got from the piranhas in the sewers. That put some fear into me. So I was the one who led the way. I went out to sniff the bodies in the courtyard and decided they were just the thing: warm, tender, with big white worms bursting with sweet juice. Almost everyone joined in. As for myself, every morning I stuck my snout into the bellies, that was the best part – it seethed and teemed in my mouth. Then I'd go roast myself in the sunshine. That took care of breakfast. It was not a good time to disturb me. There were only a few killjoys around who raised their hands to heaven and fell to their knees and told us we'd be damned. That's when I recognized my religious fanatic from the day I had my abortion. He hadn't recognized me. They were beginning to add up, all those people who refused to recognize me. I decided I should try washing now and then, in the last sink that still had a trickle of water. You had to bump and bite your way over to it, but after I'd given everyone a good scare, they basically left me alone. That's how I came to find some books behind the chipped tiles around the sink, and then I found books everywhere, it was terrible, they were even inside my mattress. I tried to eat them, at first, but they were way too dry. It took hours and hours of chewing. It was by ripping out pages to see what could be done with them that I came across Edgar's name, a name I recognized immediately from having seen it on all my posters. It started me thinking: perhaps they talked about me in the book as well? I had trouble in the beginning, and then it came back quickly, with the other letters speedily falling into line. I'll tell you just this about the book: Edgar got exactly what he deserved. I began reading all the books I kept finding, it passed the time and helped me forget my hunger – because we'd made short work of the corpses. I spent all day sitting on my behind in the attic now, and for the evenings I'd found myself a mattress, not too soiled, on which I slept off in a corner. I was taking it easy. My hair was growing back. Sometimes in the morning I'd get up too fast and bang my head on a sloping beam in the ceiling, since I was once again automatically trying to stand on my hind legs. It was while I was reading one evening that they tried to catch me. There wasn't anything at all to eat in the asylum any more, so naturally, by comparison, I must have still seemed rather appetizing. They hesitated when they found me sitting in the attic reading. It had been some time since they'd last seen me, and I must say I'd lost some weight, too. The religious fanatic was leading them. When he spotted me in the dim light, he went completely white. '*Vade retro! Vade retro!*' he shouted. Maybe he'd finally recognized me. I realized that I no longer looked so edible that they'd want to eat me up then and there, and that I'd best beat it before they got around to organizing a pigsticking party. I dashed into the courtyard and discovered that once again I ran faster on two legs than on all fours and that my breasts weren't flopping around any more. I'd carried off a book clenched in my teeth, but found I could hold it in my hand, which made it easier to breathe. I hid in what had once been the psychiatrists' dining room. There I found a white doctor's coat to wear. It revived old memories and almost brought tears of nostalgia to my eyes. In the coat pockets were a twenty euro bill and a set of keys. At nightfall I was able to open the gates incognito, and there I found, clinging to the bars, the unconscious body of the religious nut, who had collapsed from hunger. I felt sorry for him. I dragged him outside and left him in plain view in front of a church, thinking that with any luck, someone would recognize him. He still had quite a lot of life left in him, just you wait and see, but he never thanked me. And yet I saved his life. The next day, in a dustbin, I found a newspaper that expressed satisfaction with Edgar's decision to have the asylum cleaned out with a big dose of napalm. A peculiar smell still lingered in the air, and ashes floated everywhere in the neighbourhood like some kind of noxious snow. The shopkeeper from whom I bought some bread told me she was very pleased, because that *source of infection* had

been bad for business. The police were rounding up people at the end of the street, but fortunately I still had my
papers, plus I looked respectable in my white coat. I said
I was a nurse. They let me through. I could speak again,
probably from having read all those words in those
books, so you might say I'd had some practice. I sat
down in a café and finished the book I'd brought with
me, hidden under my coat. It was a book by Knut
Hamsun or whoever. It told about some missing animals
– whales, herrings – and then huge forests and people in
love and bad guys who took all their money. Personally,
I thought it was a nice book, but there was one passage
that made me feel sort of shaky, it said (I still remember
it by heart): 'Then the knife plunges in. The farmhand
gives it two little shoves to push it through the thick
skin, after which the long blade seems to melt through
the neck fat as it sinks in up to the hilt. At first the boar
doesn't understand a thing, he remains stretched out for
a few seconds, thinking about it. Aha! Then he realizes
he is being killed and utters strangled cries until he can
scream no more.' I wondered what a *boar* was; my back
began to feel all clammy. I decided to laugh it off,
because otherwise I was going to throw up. I was getting
startled looks in the café on account of my strange
laughter and people were staring at my book. I gathered
that I'd better get rid of it. Anyway that passage seemed

to me just a teensy bit *subversive*, to use a word favoured by that newspaper I'd read. Which gave me an idea. I figured that all I had to do was take the book to Edgar to join in his big clean-up campaign: I'd get myself noticed, and he'd give me a job. I had no problem finding the Censorship Bureau, it was right next to the Palace. They seemed quite stumped by my book. Nobody knew who Knut Hamsun was and I couldn't help them there. So they called a Supervisor. Me, I wanted them to call Edgar, but they told me it was absolutely impossible to disturb him over such a trifle. That annoyed me. The Supervisor appeared even more disenchanted than the others. He said that Knut Hamsun wasn't properly speaking a clear-cut case but that you couldn't say he was an enemy of Social Free Progressionism, either. And other stuff that I didn't really follow. And then he said that the iniquitous intellocratic, capitalistic, multi-ethnic regime had given the *Nobel Prize* or whatever to this Knut character, which was indisputable proof of subversion. That's how the Supervisor settled the question once and for all and was able to pack the book off to the crematory. I was impressed by the Supervisor's efficient, no-nonsense approach. I told him so and he asked me what I was doing that evening. I realized that I was in one of my better phases. I spent the entire afternoon in a hotel room trying to make myself beautiful, but the situation was deteriorating again. I figured that through the Supervisor, I would probably get to Edgar. The Supervisor looked a tad disappointed when he saw me again that evening. He invited me out to a restaurant but we didn't dawdle over the food. He kept looking at me in a funny way. Back at his place he experienced what you might call a power failure, which annoyed him so much he threw me out. My back was killing me again. As for Edgar, I'd blown it. I returned to the asylum and in the rubble I found another book that might very well – even though it was half burned to a crisp – prove dangerous if it fell into the wrong hands. I can't remember the title any more. At the Censorship Bureau, despite the fact that I'd only been there once before, they suddenly seemed to have had enough of me. One of them even held his nose. They hardly glanced at the book and tried to send me away. So I used my secret weapon. I said that I was Edgar's Egeria, his woman adviser, and that I was on all his campaign posters with him. Everybody cracked up. The Supervisor came in to see what all the noise was about. Snickering, the others explained. Then the Supervisor's face lit up, he looked into my eyes and said well of course, now he recognized me perfectly well, even though I hadn't taken very good care of myself in the meantime. I hadn't recognized him either, in his kepi and his uniform: it was the gentleman who'd extricated me from the dogs at Aqualand, my discoverer, as it were. The other employees immediately buried their noses in their files. The Supervisor took me over to the Palace, where Edgar seemed delighted to see me. He shook my hand and sent away the two masseuses. He had me given a room right there in the Palace. Reporters came and I was handed a text to memorize in which I explained how much Edgar had helped me and how he'd given a boost to my career as an actress. There were TV cameras and everything. I was to begin rehearsals the next day for a commercial in which I was replacing an actress guilty of *high treason*, but that night I got awful cramps in my back again, and they couldn't have come at a worse moment. Just when I'd got another job, I thought, it was starting all over again. The next morning, all my hair was lying on the pillow. This time I said to myself, that's it, it's cancer, I'm suffering from an *anarchic growth of cells* because I haven't lived enough *in tune with my body*. I tried to sneak off but discovered I was locked in. When Edgar's gorillas came to take me to the TV studio, they seemed pretty peeved to find me in that state. It was clear even to them that I wasn't going to cut it as a female mastermind.

'For a healthier world,' grumbled Edgar when he saw me. He sent for a doctor, who asked me if I'd been walking anywhere around *Goliath*. I didn't even know what he was talking about. It was the new nuclear power plant Edgar had had constructed. I just said that I'd worked in a perfume store and Edgar asked if maybe all those chemicals . . . The whole thing seemed to intrigue Edgar. The doctor said well, perhaps, but it would take quite a high dosage, nothing was certain, and anyway it would be prohibitively expensive. Edgar said still, it would be hilarious if they could turn the prisons into piggeries, at least they'd provide some low-cost protein. The doctor started hooting with Edgar. Personally, I've never understood anything about politics. All I know is I was happy to be in the hands of a doctor who seemed more than competent, and they sure aren't cheap. Edgar buzzed someone on an intercom and guess who showed up: the director of Perfumes Plus. He was wearing a handsome black kepi and he'd got even fatter. Unfortunately, he didn't recognize me. There must have been some big mix-up because he carted me off to a really cold prison where screams kept me awake all night. It smelled gross in there. I began having problems standing up again, and I was letting out those bellowing cries, I couldn't help it. The worst was that I never once saw the sun. After a long time – how long I couldn't say – they came to get me. Edgar in person, with all his gorillas. They seemed drunk or something. And some of the mastiffs from Aqualand were there too, and they made a big fuss over me, which did my heart good. The body-guards put a leash on me and dragged me up to the Palace while Edgar sang some outrageously smutty songs. What a swine, that Edgar. As for me, I couldn't walk at all any more. Hunger, probably. We entered a large room that was all lit up. People were dancing beneath chandeliers and there were tapestries, the kind they make nowadays, but I had eyes only for the buffet tables and the big steaming soup tureens. Everyone squealed when they caught sight of me and stopped dancing to cluster around me. They were very posh and exquisitely dressed and smelled deliciously of Yerling. Some ladies wearing Moonlight Madness designs said Edgar always had fabulous ideas for his parties, and they kept throwing their hands up, oohing and ahhing. One gentleman set a girl astride me and, weak as I was, I had to hustle around the room – up, down, across, and kitty-corner – with the girl on my back laughing herself sick to general applause. It was the first time I'd ever been the belle of a ball, but I would rather have sampled the buffet. Luckily, the girl was so drunk she finally threw up on the parquet after all that jouncing around and I managed to get a bite to eat, if you follow me. Well, now pandemonium broke out – you couldn't hear the orchestra, people were laughing so hard, and they began tossing me hunks of roast venison, slices of giraffe, whole jars of caviar, maple sugar candies, exotic African fruits, and truffles, especially truffles, they're so tasty. What a treat! They made me get up on my hind legs, stretch out my neck, and really work for my food, but those were the rules of the game. Everyone was having lots of fun. I was getting dizzy from the champagne they were pouring into me and I started feeling sentimental, shedding tears of gratitude for all the food I was getting. One lady with a stunning dress of lazuré from Gilda flung her arms around me and kissed me on both cheeks, sobbing and babbling incoherently. I would have liked to understand what she was saying, while we were both rolling around on the floor. She seemed quite fond of me. It had been a long time since anyone had shown me such affection, and I was moved to fresh tears. 'Look at that!' the lady stammered. 'She's crying!' And then the crowd formed a circle around me while the orchestra played the bunny hop or some old retro thing like that. The upper crust certainly knows how to party. By now devilled eggs and caviar were squashed all over the floor; people were skidding as they waltzed. Edgar had had a girl stripped of her clothes and he absolutely insisted that I sniff her rear end – he was always a stitch, that Edgar. And then the orchestra abruptly stopped playing and a bodyguard touched Edgar's arm. Edgar stood up as best he could, suddenly recovered some of his dignity, and announced, 'My dear friends, it's midnight!' Everyone yelled and I wondered if it was the end of the world or something, but they all hugged and kissed one another, and I wound up covered with lipstick: Yerling, Gilda, and Moonlight Madness, too – nothing trashy about this crowd. We heard twelve loud peals from the bell in the cathedral Edgar had had built on the site of the Arc de Triomphe. Then more champagne corks popped. I myself could not drink another drop; I was beginning to feel nauseated after that long period of privation in prison. I kept slipping on the polished floor all coated with muck, banging my face and scraping my dugs. People were laughing but I wasn't the star of the show any more, you could tell they were getting bored. Edgar brought in the second major attraction. Well, I thought, for once I'm off the hook, I was more than pleased to be low on sex appeal at that moment, as I was so wiped out I would have been useless. The pretty young thing Edgar had produced was struggling and whimpering. She was just a child, really, and didn't hold up too well. When they'd all finished having their fun with her she started wandering around the room on her hands and knees with her eyes completely rolled back in her head, probably from being tuckered out and new to this sort of thing. Knowing

Edgar, I was sure she wouldn't leave empty handed, and I'd have liked to go comfort her but I just couldn't get a single intelligible sound out of my mouth. One of the gorillas hauled the kid into an adjacent room, where I saw him amuse himself with her a bit and then put a bullet in her head. I was disappointed with him. He was lucky Edgar hadn't seen that or he'd have been in hot water. Other girls and even boys were brought in to party with us. The slippery parquet began to get sticky with all that blood, which sort of helped me regain my balance, at least. I felt sorry for the boys – they're not so used to it – and I started gnawing on the bonds of a boy who'd been left in the lurch: no one was paying attention to him any more and he was shrieking because of something burning him up his bum or whatever. I should have left well enough alone. You'll never believe this but some guy noticed me next to the boy and began pulling some rotten stuff on me. I tried to make him understand that he was mistaken, that I wasn't like that at all, but nothing doing. My mulishness earned me a taste of the whip, but I didn't care, I'd acquired a thick hide. Right when everyone seemed to be enjoying themselves the most, the orchestra stopped playing again. In came my marabout, beautifully outfitted in white and wearing his native costume once more, but now his skin was very light. From close up you could see that those

Moonlight Madness bleaching creams hadn't quite been perfected yet; his skin was all mottled. The marabout said, 'Repent, brothers,' and he waved some sort of large golden spiral at everybody. The whole crowd fell flat on their faces; some women crawled to the marabout to kiss the hem of his garment, while other people had shaking fits. It would have been a lovely scene, truly touching, if there had been complete silence, like the kind you get in cathedrals, but my tummy was growling from all that food and it was so embarrassing I almost died. Fortunately for me there was a girl strung up to a chandelier by her hair who was making even more of a racket. Her insides were hanging out, bowels and all – they'd had a fine time with her. In his great goodness, the marabout cut down the girl and blessed the others who were lying around. Gesturing to have all that cleaned up, he said, 'Now go home, my brothers, prepare yourselves spiritually for the coming Third Millennium, and pray that the spirit of the Spiral will wisely inspire our blessed leader.' I saw Edgar bend down to kiss the hem of the marabout's robe, and taking the enormous golden spiral in both arms, he raised it over the heads of the crowd. Then he dismissed all those prostrate people in evening clothes with a wave of his hand. The marabout had come a long way since the days of Perfumes Plus, although it is true that at that time the most eminent dignitaries were already making pilgrimages to his loft in the African quarter. Some drowsy-looking cleaning women arrived with buckets and brooms. I heard the marabout talking to Edgar about a ceremony in the cathedral; poor Edgar wasn't going to get much sleep. Day was breaking, scattering lovely reflections across the parquet and the gilt furniture; it gave me quite a turn, seeing the sun rise. A cleaning woman found me behind a tapestry and said, 'What do we do with this, Monsieur Edgar?' Edgar, who has always cherished the common folk, saw fit to reply, 'That's my New Year's gift to the Palace employees.' I saw that poor woman's face light up, and I've got to say she was nothing but skin and bones. 'Oh thank you, thank you, Monsieur Edgar,' she said. But I had no intention of giving up without a fight – I mean really, who did they think I was? I began grunting ferociously and I saw the marabout look in my direction. 'Edgar,' he said laughingly, 'wherever did you get a pig in this day and age?' 'You know,' replied Edgar, 'I've got connections everywhere.' They both chuckled. 'All joking aside,' whispered Edgar (but I had sharp ears), 'it's a rather interesting case, perhaps caused by Goliath, or maybe a cocktail of toxic effects. I should have my scientists look into it. Do you realize what the long-term possibilities could be?' Edgar started to cackle, but the marabout looked suddenly grave. 'I've seen this kind of witchcraft before, in my country,' he observed. 'Don't be silly,' said Edgar, 'let's not start that again – the Spiral is the Prozac of the people.' And he snickered. 'It has nothing to do with the Spiral,' said the marabout solemnly. He came over to me and gently patted my snout. 'How are you, sweetie?' he asked me, and it warmed my heart to know that he'd recognized me. 'One day I'll introduce you to the owner of Moonlight Madness,' the marabout continued to Edgar, 'and you'll be in for a big surprise.' 'I hate surprises,' remarked Edgar wearily, 'but I do like to be astonished. If you can do that I'll have you named Commander of the Faithful instead of that imbecile Marchepiède, but leave that pig alone, it amuses me.' So just imagine, both these VIPs began tickling me behind the ears – the marabout promising Edgar some excellent sausage from the Antilles, and Edgar promising the marabout this business of being Commander of the Faithful, and neither of them wanted to let me go. I was extremely tickled. 'I'll give it back to you,' the marabout finally said, and he did something to Edgar with his hand, I don't know what, so that Edgar went all funny and let go of my tail. I pranced off proudly with the marabout – he was my favourite of the two, after all.

'I told you to come see me earlier,' said the marabout,

sitting in the back of his chauffeured car. 'Look at the state you're in now!' I was a little ashamed, it's true. We arrived at his place – he'd taken a larger loft in the business district – and he gave me an upstairs room all to myself, requesting that I please not crap it up. From then on, the marabout busied himself each day concocting ointments for me, massaging me all over, making me drink potions. He had the last rhinoceros in Africa killed for me, to obtain some powdered horn – would you believe it, with what that stuff costs. I was turning green, blue, but the marabout was never satisfied. Although my corkscrew tail was gradually withering, the ears and snout were hanging on. I just left him to it. Room and board in the lap of luxury, what more could you ask. I started devouring all the marabout's books but they were really too scary; they talked about zombies, men changed into wild animals, unsolved mysteries in the tropics. Some crazy things go on down there. It must be the climate. Anyway, it made the marabout laugh to see me browsing in his bookcases, and we got along famously. I gradually regained the power of speech, which was nice, and the two of us could chatter away. You could say I was getting better – my hair was growing back, I could almost walk upright, I had five fingers again on my front hooves. The marabout's lady friend was a touch jealous, though; she told him he was going to have problems with the Society for the Protection of Animals, keeping an animal in his home like that. This friend was that lady of a certain age who was always weeping in the little park, former bosom buddy of my murdered client, if you follow me. The lady had very quickly found consolation with this African marabout, and him a man, too. You just never can tell about people. She told him that the SPA had now become quite influential: it seems that an erstwhile actress pal of Edgar's had snagged the post of Secretary of Public Morals in the Department of the Interior, and she wasn't kidding, that actress. 'Nowadays,' said the marabout's lady friend dolefully, 'the defenders of human rights are in prison.' Glancing around uneasily, the marabout whispered to her not to say that so loud. 'In any case,' he said in a booming voice, 'our dear Edgar has found a radical way to get rid of the rabble.' And he looked at me in a sort of preoccupied way. I was touched to see him worry about me like that. He was slaving away to find an *antidote*. He was convinced something was very wrong with me, so naturally, he had me worried. And then all that gunk he had me swallow probably wasn't too great for my health. The marabout kept saying he'd get there, he'd find something, he'd figure it out, or if all else failed, he knew someone to whom he could send me. But the lady friend wanted me out of there, and fast. I must say that once I was standing upright and talking and so on, the marabout and I started fooling around again. He told his friend that I was an *exceptional individual*, think of that. Alas, luck was never on my side, and this happy interlude came to an end. A commando unit of the SPA burst into the loft one morning to arrest the marabout and his friend. Marchepiède was the one who became Commander of the Faithful. I know, because he's the one who dealt with me afterwards. Marchepiède – no reason why I shouldn't tell you now – was the raving lunatic from the day of my abortion, the weirdo I rescued from the asylum and all, so you can see the sort of people we have for leaders. Edgar didn't seem all that much in charge any more – I don't think Marchepiède could swallow his having preferred a black guy to run the cathedral or something. There weren't many blacks in the streets any more, and I had no idea what had happened to the marabout. Marchepiède tried everything he could think of on me, he said he was sceptical. Although Edgar assured him that I wasn't what I seemed, Marchepiède refused to believe it. He said it wasn't God-in-Heaven possible. Did I ever get exorcized! The whole cathedral was reserved just for yours truly. They swatted me with spirals and crosses, and they even went on to whips and lots of other excitement, even in my more fetching moments. I would come out of these sessions a total wreck. Edgar repeated his story so often he wore out his welcome; I think that's why Marchepiède had him confined, if you recall. There was a lot of talk about Edgar's mental illness. It seems he was neighing and eating nothing but grass, down on all fours. Poor Edgar. Well, you know about the rest. War broke out and so forth, there was the Epidemic, and then that series of famines. I'd spent all this time hidden in the crypt of the cathedral – I mean, what if they'd found me. I'd have brought five thousand euros a pound on the black market, easy, no bones about it. When I emerged, everyone had forgotten about me. In any case, I don't know what happened to Marchepiède and the others, I haven't read a newspaper in a long time. All was calm again, you could feel it in the streets. I had no idea where to go. The only address I remembered, aside from Honoré's – but could you see me going back there? – was the marabout's loft. I went to his place. Well, can you imagine, there he was, and his lady friend as well. They'd both aged terribly. The marabout had these whitish growths on his skin, tumours that made him look like an old elephant. I could see in their eyes that I was in good shape again, probably from my long rest in the crypt. They welcomed me as though I'd come back from the dead. The marabout hugged me but begged me to leave them in peace now, saying he couldn't do anything more for me. He gave me another address and off I went.

The owner and managing director of Moonlight Madness greeted me warmly when I told him the marabout had sent me. The director was extraordinarily handsome, even more so than Honoré. He sniffed my rear end instead of shaking my hand, but aside from that he couldn't have been nicer, a truly refined man, well dressed and everything. He told me he'd heard a lot about me and was familiar with my problem. It was a relief not to have to tell him anything, because I was looking pretty foxy at the time, but I was afraid it wouldn't last. The director poured me a Bloody Mary and explained that this sort of thing came and went – one day you were like everyone else, the next you found yourself braying or roaring, it depended, but willpower was the key to holding your own. The director explained to me that in his own case, he'd managed to regulate his life by the Moon. I'd never thought of that. Then he asked me what I was doing that evening. He clearly found me attractive, and he was so good-looking, so sweet, I thought I was dreaming. He said now that the quays along the Seine had been rebuilt, they were delightful in the Moonlight, and he knew a marvellous restaurant. He gave me a big smile. He had two divinely pearly canines just peeking out from between his lips, and a thin blond moustache that reached all the way to his ear-lobes. He was so cute I nearly fell over backwards. We were strolling along the quays of the Seine when the director of Moonlight Madness (his first name was Yvan) looked down at me and exclaimed, as though he were gasping, 'Run away, quickly!' We'd had a lovely evening, so I didn't understand. But when I saw the look that suddenly came over his face, I took to my heels. I hid behind a tree and watched, since I couldn't bear to run out on such a wild guy. He sat down on a bench and put his head in his hands. He looked so weary. A long moment passed. The Moon came out from behind some clouds right above the ruins of the Pont-Neuf, and the effect was striking. There were zigzags of white light on the water, and the flying buttresses or whatever that were still standing on the Ile gleamed brightly against the dark sky. Well, it had been some time since I'd been out for a walk along the river. The Palace had been completely destroyed, but all those huge arches lying jumbled on the ground and those fallen statues and that sort of skeletal pyramid you glimpsed through the massive gap – they were charming in the Moonlight, in my opinion, a thrilling sight, all pale and chalky. At that point I'd almost forgotten my Yvan. I heard a muffled cry over by the bench. Yvan was standing, gazing up at the Moon and shaking his fist at it. That gave me a shock. And then Yvan fell on all fours. His back arched. His clothes split apart all down his spine, revealing long, bristly grey fur. His body swelled, ripping the material across his shoulders and at his wrists. Yvan's face was distorted, elongated and pointy, glistening with slaver and sparkling teeth, while dense fur now entirely covered his shoulders. The Moon was in Yvan's eyes, like the pallid gleam of an icy stare. You felt he was suffering, you could hear him panting. His hands clutched at the ground as if the knotty, stumpy fingers had sunk their claws deep into the soil. It was as though Yvan's hands couldn't tear themselves away yet wanted to make the earth pay, to rip out its guts. Yvan's shoulders shuddered violently and his hind end shook like an uprooted tree. His shoes exploded, his hands tore at the earth, and dirt flew everywhere. Yvan's entire body leapt into motion. He stalked along, enormous, writhing in the Moonlight. Something howled inside him. It came up from his belly the way I scream when I smell death. The Moon grew dim. All the ruins around us stood petrified, so to speak, and the river stopped flowing. Yvan howled again. I couldn't move; my blood had run cold. I wasn't even frightened any more. My heart and all my muscles felt dead. I heard the world stop living at Yvan's howl, as if the whole history of the world were tied up in that sound, everything that has ever happened to us – I don't quite know how to put it. Someone was coming. Yvan didn't turn a hair: he pounced. This someone, he didn't believe what he'd heard, you could sense his excitement in the air. And then you couldn't sense anything at all. A thrill of horror: nothing more. Not even a yelp. Yvan danced around the body. It was astonishing to see Yvan so light, capering beneath the Moon, flicking his silvery tail at the sky like the flickering of a cheery bonfire. The whole broken mass of his body and the pain of his first movements had vanished beneath his Moonstruck fur, beneath the precision of his slashing fangs, beneath his leaps, his savage entrechats, his big white grins. I fell stark raving madly in love with Yvan. I didn't dare come out yet; I waited until he'd eaten his fill. When I saw him licking his chops and washing his paws at the edge of the water, when I saw that he'd lapped up almost all the blood, I approached him quietly. Yvan looked at me. 'That's better,' he said. I understood that I could draw closer. I wrapped my arms around Yvan's neck and kissed him inside each ear: it was soft, it was warm. Yvan rolled on the ground and I scratched him below his breastbone. I lay down on him to enjoy his fine smell. I kissed him on the neck, I kissed him on the corner of his mouth, I licked his teeth, I bit his tongue. Yvan laughed gleefully, licked me everywhere, reared up over me, and

I rolled over on my back. We both began whimpering, we were so happy. Then Yvan sat on his rump and I lay down between his paws. We stayed that way for a very long time, letting ourselves float along on our joy. I kept looking at Yvan, propping myself up on my elbows, smiling at him, and he smiled back. Yvan was silver grey, with a long muzzle that was both strong and delicate; he had a virile face, noble and elegant; large paws, well furred; and a very broad, velvety soft chest. Yvan was the incarnation of beauty. The sun had begun to rise and Yvan fell asleep with his snout on his paws. I stayed sitting next to him, watching over him; any passers by might very well think he was my dog, a great big dog. That idea made me smile, filled me with tender feelings. The sun glinted on the Seine in pale yellow reflections as the Moon faded away. A golden haze enveloped the ruins of the Palace, blurring its outlines, like a superfine powder sifting down, a dusting of light falling gently everywhere. You couldn't look directly at the last remaining shards of glass on the pyramid, they glittered so. It was like a veil of gold tossed over the girders. I felt Yvan stir against my knees. Something strange came over me when I saw Yvan almost dissolve in the sunshine that streaked his muzzle with fuzzy lines, tamed his wild eyes, erased his ears, shaved off his fur. Yvan glittered – you could hardly see him in the halo that surrounded and obliterated him. I thought he was going to dwindle slowly away in my arms, and I shouted and clung to him. But it happened very gently. The brilliance of the sun's rays subsided as they touched the remaining walls of the old cathedral. Yvan lifted his head and I saw the face of a man. He stood up, holding out his hand to me. 'Let's go,' he said. He was buck naked and I was laughing like a hyena. We walked back to his apartment. Luckily, the streets were almost empty, and anyway, ever since Edgar, people had seen lots worse than that.

Then began the most wonderful period of my life. It makes my heart ache to think back on it now. Poor Yvan. We lived together for several months in his apartment. On each full Moon, Yvan went out for a snack. He'd shown me how to adapt my own cycle to the fluctuations of the Moon, but I wasn't nearly as good at it as he was – I think he really had it in his blood. He figured that my hormonal swings were messing things up (he didn't know all that much about female matters). The main thing was to rev up a lot of willpower. When I'd had enough of being a sow, if it had gone on for too long or was inconvenient for some reason, I'd shut myself up in our bedroom and do breathing exercises, concentrating as hard as I could. I still concentrate like that when I'm trying to hold my pen correctly and improve my handwriting, but ever since Yvan died it's been getting harder and harder. Besides, what difference can it make to me now if I'm a pig? I don't see anyone any more except a few others like me, and just the thought of going back to the city tires me out. The best times with Yvan were when I was in heat. We were very careful not to shout too much, because of the neighbours, but did we ever have fun! Yvan loved me equally well as a woman and as a sow. He said it was fantastic to have two modes of being, two females for the price of one, in a way, and what a time we had. Yvan had retired completely from the business world to enjoy our new life to the fullest, and he'd sold Moonlight Madness to Yerling, so we were rolling in money. Yvan dressed me in the most beautiful clothes. He'd even made an enormous donation to the Free Citizens' Government to rebuild the Pont-Neuf, in memory of our first night. We used to go for strolls there when I was presentable enough to be seen in the street. It always made me terribly proud to see the plaque with Yvan's name on the Pont-Neuf. Unfortunately, they never finished rebuilding the bridge, and only Yvan was able to leap across to the other bank on nights when the Moon was full – he was unbelievably strong. A great deal of Yvan's money had been embezzled, there was a huge scandal, but Yvan said he didn't want to get involved, that the Pont-Neuf was fine the way it was. People didn't understand. It wasn't very practical from a traffic point of view, admittedly, so it was a good thing the Ministry had the idea of using the breach in the former Palace to put through an urban highway. All right, it did kind of spoil the view, and Yvan thought about intervening, but he had deliberately withdrawn almost completely from social and political life. He turned his back on everything to devote himself exclusively to me. Once in a while we ran into a few paparazzi on our walks along the Pont-Neuf; Yvan wouldn't let me read the articles because they weren't very kind to me, it seems, I never looked good in the photos, and they called me a *fat pig* – Yvan and I had good laughs over that. I simply can't tell you how little I cared about all that at the time. If people were jealous because the famous Yvan of Moonlight Madness had given up everything for a fat pig, that was their problem. They just didn't understand. Especially since it was around then that the death of the marabout was reported in the newspapers. Some experts started looking into those old skin-bleaching creams from Moonlight Madness, so Yvan was glad he'd already put himself out to pasture. He used his contacts at the Ministry to cover up the affair, and he gave all his Yerling stock to the marabout's lady friend. We began travelling. Sometimes it was a trifle complicated, because with all the disruption, the exotic foods, the air conditioning, the monsoon or what-have-you, I couldn't manage to keep my shape human enough for us to leave our hotel room. But it was quite exciting for us both to stay shut up like that, lying under the mosquito netting while reporters aired the most preposterous conjectures about our absence. In the end we had to venture out. Yvan, who'd been famous for his eccentricities, gave me a diamond collar: we strolled around together, with Yvan walking me on a leash. I was his pet pig the way others have a Pekingese or a boa. We never could have done that in Paris – Yvan would have had too many problems with the SPA, and we couldn't risk having me confiscated and winding up in a pigsty or worse. That's why we stayed abroad so much. Plus it was convenient for nights when there was a full Moon, since nobody keeps track of blacks or Chinese the way they do with Parisians. It was too bad we wound up having to return to Paris when those idiotic Free Citizens quarrelled with the whole world over their ideas about communal autarky (thank goodness Yvan had sold Moonlight Madness in time). Life became a touch more compli- cated because the people Yvan had known in the gov- ernment had been imprisoned – it was that whole period of the Great Trials, I'm sure you remember. The New Citizens decided to complete the reconstruction of the

Pont-Neuf and tried to conscript us for compulsory
labour, along with everyone else. They drained most of
Yvan's bank accounts and actually showed up at our
doorstep – we couldn't believe it. By some good fortune,
Yvan had kept enough cash squirrelled away to grease
everyone's paws, or we'd have been dead ducks. I suppose it was all this stress that kept me a pig three quar-
ters of the time. We became more and more secretive. It
wasn't unpleasant, far from it. We stayed in our lovely
apartment without being bothered any more, since Yvan
had made some new contacts. He procured fruits and
vegetables for me through an Internet network dis-
guised as a cultural database, via a flourishing black
market. He bought red meat for himself, and we were
able to live in perfect autarky. We just had to be extra
careful during the deliveries, so I hid in the bedroom.
Our days passed delightfully. At dawn, while the entire
city was still asleep, we were awakened by the exchange
of coolness and warmth between the Moon and the sun,
and by puffs of wind from the stars plunging down to
the other side of the world. Yvan would lick me behind
the ears, take deep breaths of fresh air at the window,
then go juice my potatoes while I still lazed in bed. We'd
caress each other. Then when the sky had become a
wash of gold, we'd lie sprawled out on the veranda, sun-
ning ourselves, and during the day we took several

naps, contented as cats. We had our books delivered, and newspapers, too, and then we stopped even that. So when everyone began talking about the series of murders on the quays, we never heard a thing. We'd thought that given all the unrest, no one would notice a few extra bodies lying around, but those asses the Citizens had managed their takeover fairly well and they'd organized a terrifically efficient police force. I think it was the way the corpses' throats were cut that intrigued them so much. I've read the articles since then, where they talked about the *Full-Moon Maniac*, or *The Beast*, I mean I ask you. Some of them laid it on thick with their *punishment* and their *redemption*, but they got zapped right away. This was no laughing matter to the Citizens. In the clippings I kept you can see the heads of the corpses, all neatly decapitated the way Yvan liked to do it. I can safely say that they never knew what hit them. The investigators lost a lot of time searching for the murder weapon; they simply couldn't believe it was an animal, naturally, since there hadn't been any wild animals wandering around Paris for some time, as you can imagine. *Rationality* is the ruination of mankind, you can take it from me. We got wind of all this uproar from a delivery boy. Yvan decided to play dead at home, but that's when things started getting tough for us. The first full Moon in particular was a very trying experience. Yvan began going around in circles. He'd stopped talking to me. I turned on the television to try to take my mind off the situation, but I couldn't help keeping a discreet eye on Yvan. He sat on the floor, facing the window, and stared fixedly at the Moon. Me, I kept my eyes on his hair, mostly – that was always the first sign. And his hair started going grey, as though he'd aged ten years in one instant. Then his hair stood on end and began sticking up out of his collar, between his shirt buttons, on his cheeks and the back of his hands. 'Use your willpower, Yvan,' I said grimly. His Yerling suit split right down the back – he used to go through so many of them! His spine arched grotesquely; he looked like a dromedary. Then came the rest of the horror show, the swelling paws, the claws, the pointy ears, the teeth taking over – it took some getting used to, I'm telling you. Yvan in such a state was truly an arresting sight. When he turned to me and I saw the crazed look in his eyes, I felt this burning pain in my belly; I'd never seen him this way in our home. I thought, 'Time to call Pronto Pizza.' I dashed to the phone. Luckily, they're easy to memorize, those three-digit emergency numbers, because sometimes it's a question of life or death. Trembling, I blurted out an order for our salvation: 'Hello – send a pizza to 7 Quai des Grands-Augustins, quick!' I knew that Pronto Pizza never takes more than twenty minutes. For Yvan and me, they were the longest twenty minutes of our lives. I'd shut myself up in the bedroom, where I could hear Yvan howling and scratching at the door, then crying as only wolves do, and cursing the Earth in long, drawn-out wails. Yvan's suffering was appalling. I strove to remain calm, as it was not the moment for me to fall apart as well. Quietly, I opened the bedroom door. I spoke to Yvan. I emerged, if I may put it this way, as warily as a wolf. Yvan's eyes never left me. I approached him very, very carefully and took his head in my hands very, very gently. Seated, Yvan came up to my shoulders. I felt a shiver go clear down his spine. I saw something like a gleam of humanity flicker across his eyes, and his irises contracted with the pain of fighting against his instinct. I saw love struggling with hunger in Yvan's eyes. I began speaking softly to him. I spoke of the steppes, the summer snows on the taiga, the forests of Gaul, the Basque hills, the sheepfolds of the Cevennes, the Scottish moors, the wind and the rain. I ran down the long list of all his dead brothers, gave the names of every pack. I talked about the Great Beast of the Gévaudan, and the last wolves, those who hide out in the ruins of the Bronx and whom no one dares approach. I evoked the dreams of children and the nightmares of men. I spoke to him of the Earth. I don't know where I was getting all this, it just came to me, from the depths of my being, and I had no trouble finding even the hardest and most obscure words. That's why I'm writing now, because I remember everything Yvan gave me that evening, and everything I gave him. Moaning faintly, Yvan curled up and fell half asleep. I watched dreams flutter beneath his silken eyelids. And then I felt as though my insides were being ripped out: the Moon tore us apart, rising to its zenith and flooding the room with blue light. Yvan sprang up. He heard the blood humming in my veins, smelled the flesh beneath my skin, saw the carotid artery pulsing in my neck. His yellow irises split in two, and letting out a great howl, he crouched to spring. The fur rose on his back, his tail stiffened; I could see the nerves, tendons, veins standing out in his throat and all the way down to his gnarled paws. Well, I thought, it's a lovely way to die. Just then the doorbell rang. Startled, Yvan turned towards the sound. I didn't even have time to say hello to the delivery man. The pizza spurted up into the air. You couldn't tell the blood from the tomato sauce. I decided there was no doubt about it: home delivery was incredibly convenient.

After that we had dinner delivered regularly, every evening on the full Moon. I ate the pizza, Yvan ate the pizza man. And he had to eat every last morsel, to avoid causing a stench, so Yvan grew plump, cute as could be. We sampled every pizzeria in Paris, to cover our tracks: Speedo Pizza, Flash Pizza, Whizzo Pizza, Vroom Vroom Pizza, Faster Pizza, etc. We'd have the deliveries sent to fake addresses. Yvan used false names to rent studio apartments for the occasion. Getting rid of the vehicles was another problem, but that's what the Seine is for. We'd wait for a moonless night, and splash! We really lived a life of adventure, another Bonnie and Clyde. On the one hand, our everyday existence was quite pleasant; we had a superb apartment, love – and then once a month there was a new trap to set, different situations to deal with, new sensory experiences, fresh smells, exotically tasty deliveries. The Los Angeles disaster had sent a new variety of immigrant hurrying off to Paris, where they all specialized in fast-food pizza, and these newcomers were delicious, according to Yvan: nice and fat, with just the slightest aftertaste of Coca Cola. Perhaps it's class snobbery, but Yvan always enjoyed junk food. I was growing somewhat bored, though, and that's why I began watching television more often. I was quite upset by *Vanished Without a Trace*. I should have listened to Yvan, who hated that kind of audience-pandering stuff. The show was very popular because of all the people who'd disappeared, what with the War and the Great Trials. My mother turned up on the programme. I'd completely forgotten her. Well, she hadn't forgotten me. She was holding issues of *The Parisian Inquirer* and *Heartache*; photos of Yvan and me paraded in close-up across the screen. My mother sobbed so lustily you could hardly hear her saying that she'd recognized me and wanted to see her dear little girl again. Then, to my utter consternation, pictures of me as a child filled the screen, even snapshots of my mother breastfeeding me. Yvan was rolling on the floor in stitches, poor dear – if he'd only known where this thing would lead us. My mother said my father had died during the war – I racked my brains trying to remember him – and that she was unemployed, without means of support, homeless, basically, and that the least I could do was get in touch with her. The host of the programme made a big deal out of my liaison with Yvan, saying that the rich were eating us out of house and home and would leave us without so much as a pot to piss in. I thought Yvan was going to die laughing. When he'd managed to settle down, we tried to talk it over calmly, the two of us, and Yvan said that all my mother wanted was money. That was the first time we'd ever had an argument. Yvan told me it was most unlikely that my mother's house out in the country (the one she'd bought with her Lotto winnings) had been destroyed in the war, that she certainly wasn't out on the street, and that she must have some money still stashed away. Me, I must admit that that TV show really threw me for a loop – I don't know whether it was seeing my mother again, or the photos of me when I was little, or what I looked like now in close-up on the TV screen. I couldn't stand it that Yvan was talking that way. I told him he didn't have a clue what it was like to be poor and hungry, and other hogwash along those lines. When I think back on it, I feel terrible that I was so angry with Yvan over so little. At the time we had no idea that our days of happiness were numbered. Yvan sulked and announced that he was prepared to send some money to my mother, but that seeing her again would get us into endless trouble. He was well aware that when all was said and done, the Citizens were after his hide. This hullabaloo on TV made him nervous. He figured they were bribing my mother to lure the wolf from the woods, so to speak. Hearing Yvan talk like that, with such heartless logic, made me cry. Yvan tried to explain to me that this show was a set-up, that it suited everybody to pretend that the defendants at the Trials were perhaps still alive, but I never did understand politics at all, and I shouted back that it concerned only my mother and me. Yvan wasn't putting himself in my place: my father, mother, and I, we'd lived in those lousy housing projects in Garenne-le-Mouillé for years and years – he had no idea what it was like – and I felt sorry for my mother. I was getting all mixed up, unable to think straight, seeing myself on TV every evening like that. A voiceover would explain that I still hadn't got in touch with my mother, and we'd see a photo of me as a little girl, one of my mother in Garenne-le-Mouillé, then pictures of me and Yvan. It killed me to see how frumpy I'd got, and it killed me to think my mother had recognized me in spite of that. Maternal instinct is a wonderful thing, a *gut feeling*, as they say. Seeing me like this put Yvan's back up: he told me that I was a lot dumber than he'd ever imagined. We used to yell our heads off. Yvan would walk the streets of Paris at night, coming home drunk and soaked through; I'm not too sure what he was getting up to. Our sole remaining moments of true togetherness revolved around the pizza delivery man. The detectives of *Vanished Without a Trace* were starting to close in on us, and the Quai des Grands-Augustins wasn't exactly an inconspicuous address. I must admit – how it pains me to remember! – that I telephoned the TV show a few times, they put my mother on the line, and I always hung up at the last minute. Today I wonder if they didn't trace us to the Quai des Grands-Augustins through these repeated phone calls. The station would broadcast tapes of my hellos being cut off, which made me feel wretchedly guilty, plus I could see that they were using my ungainly physique to make everyone dislike me. My mother showed up a few times during 'They Are Still Alive', a feature on the programme, to weep and call my name. I swear, it was just awful. You could see the ratings appear in red on the screen and they were the highest ever registered on the meter. You get the idea. Yvan tossed the TV into the Seine and we decided to move. But Yvan loved the Seine too much, and we couldn't bring ourselves to do the smart thing by leaving Paris. Even though the borders were closed, we could have at least left for the countryside. We'd both still be there today. The new apartment we'd picked out was right on the other side of the Seine, near where the Pont Mirabeau used to be. The detectives from *Vanished Without a Trace* lost track of us temporarily, and since our ratings meter score dropped when the mother of the director of Perfumes Plus became the new star, they finally gave up on us. We weren't mentioned much any more, and I had no more news of my mother. It was like a vacation for me. I did manage to follow the programme on the little portable TV set from the Mercedes, because I wanted to find out if my former boss's mother was going to find her son, but Yvan and I got back together again anyway and were able to enjoy a few moments of happiness. Then things began to happen fast. I don't like leaving my lair, and I was naturally rather upset the day we moved, so I was a complete pig:

snout, trotters, protruding rump – simply impossible to disguise. Yvan had to cram me into a large bag, but when I'm a sow I get really claustrophobic and I couldn't stand it in there. As he was parking the Mercedes, I panicked and jumped out of the bag. We'd been careful to move at twilight, when it's hard to see shapes clearly, but someone must have noticed us anyhow, and a neighbour probably turned us in. The SPA arrived in the dead of night. It was just our bad luck that there was a full moon. Yvan had eaten and was sleeping as soundly as a dormouse while I dozed beside him, stuffed with pizza. I don't remember any more what shape I was in, my recollections are understandably confused, but when I heard, 'Open up! SPA!' I felt my corkscrew tail pop right out. If I hadn't been so beastly emotional, Yvan might still be alive today, they'd simply have carted me off for questioning. The SPA broke down the door and surrounded us with their machine guns. Yvan woke up snarling. The SPA couldn't get over finding such a big wolf and a pig together, and in a Parisian apartment to boot. All traces of the delivery man were gone, except for the motorbike downstairs, but that wasn't the problem. If only we'd rented a little studio for the delivery that night, the way we'd always done before! But with our brand-new address near the Pont Mirabeau, we hadn't bothered with our usual precautions so soon. Poor us. Me, I was secretly telling Yvan to stay calm, whatever he did; what with all he had in his stomach, I was hoping that at least hunger wouldn't make him edgy and that he'd let himself be led quietly away. The SPA people had never seen anything like this, however, and they were scared. Some woman in a uniform walked around the apartment drawing up a report, and I know that the newspapers the next day said that Yvan, the former owner of Moonlight Madness, had left wild animals alone in his home in the heart of Paris – thereby offering a prime example of the depravity of the rich, whose fault it is the sewers are swarming with crocodiles – and fled who knows where with his mistress. Journalists never understand anything about anything. The SPA guys still had their guns aimed at Yvan when that woman finished writing her report and said, 'Okay, let's start with the pig.' One guy came over to me with a big net while another lassoed me around the neck. Yvan attacked, and shots rang out as his fangs sank in. Yvan had time to decapitate two or three of them before crawling into a corner to die. And I died with him. I tried to lie down on Yvan and weep but I tripped in the mesh of the net. They put me in a van and then in a cage at the zoo. I screamed for several days. I wasn't eating. Visitors would toss me peanuts and French fries, and on a greasy piece of newspaper I saw the last photo of Yvan. He was stuffed, in the entrance hall of the Museum of Natural History. I lay down to await death. I remember that children threw firecrackers at me through the bars. A crowd of vets busied themselves around me, giving me injections; a marabout came to rub ointments on me and said he'd never seen a pig in such condition. I think they left me for dead in the end, and I wound up in a refrigerated truck, going off to the slaughterhouse, I suppose. It was the cold that brought me around. I was stark naked, in my human form once more. Perhaps that was because I'd hit bottom. I stood up and simply turned the inside handle on the door, which opened; I waited for a red light and jumped out. I lifted up a sewer grating and escaped down there, where it was warm and no one would see me. I just had to watch out for the crocodiles. I found a passage leading into the catacombs and came out under the Museum of Natural History: I wanted to bid one last farewell to Yvan. That's something I don't feel like talking about. Then I knocked out one of the night-shift employees with his own broom and stole his African boubou. I phoned the TV station and asked for the host of *Vanished Without a Trace*, explaining that I had information about Yvan's mistress. They gave me the host's phone number. I called him and told him who I was. He invited me right over to his place, and I went there with the broomstick. I'm the one who killed the host of *Vanished Without a Trace*. I rummaged through his things and saw my mother's address in a folder and I left with all the money I could find. I took a train at dawn.

To be on the safe side, I climbed into a cattle car. I felt a little better with cows around. I drank some milk. I relaxed and slept a lot. When the train reached its destination, I was wavering between my two states. I'd feel quite cold in my boubou as my skin grew thinner, and when it thickened, I wouldn't feel a thing any more. The boubou was ripping everywhere. I stole hay from the cows, eating bales of it to prepare for what lay ahead. I left the cattle car at nightfall and quickly reached the outskirts of the little town. I kept belching from the hay because I don't know how to ruminate and hay is rather hard on the digestion. I had to stop often, too, because I had the runs, partly from not having eaten in such a long time. I decided I was hardly in a fit state to go see my mother, especially in my tattered boubou. My mother's not too fond of eccentricities. I reached the last streets outside the town and saw bare trees swaying slowly in the wind. I thought perhaps I'd wait a bit before ringing my mother's doorbell. I was nervous. I went over to the trees. It was the first time I'd ever seen trees that tall, trees that smelled so good. They smelled of bark, of sap gathered in at the base of the trunk, and all the slumbering strength of winter. The ground around the thick roots was loose, crumbly, as though they were kneading it as they plunged deeply into the soil. I buried my nose in it. It smelled wonderfully of last autumn's dead leaves and broke up into small, brittle clumps scented with moss, acorns, mushrooms. I dug, I scrabbled – that odour was like the whole planet entering my body, conjuring up in me seasons, flights of wild geese, snowdrops, fruits, the south wind. All the strata of all the seasons were in those layers of humus. The scent grew clearer, closing in on something. I found a big black truffle and at first I thought of that New Year's Eve in 2000 when I'd pigged out at that orgy, and then the memory faded; when I bit into the truffle, the perfume went from my nose to my throat and made it seem as though I were eating a morsel of the Earth. All the winter of the Earth exploded in my mouth: I no longer remembered either the millennium to come or any of my experiences – everything rolled up into a ball inside me and I forgot it all. I lost my memory, I have no idea for how long. I ate and ate. The truffles tasted like ponds when they freeze, like huddled buds waiting for spring, like shoots straining in the frigid ground, like the patient vigour of future harvests. I felt the weight of winter in my belly, a longing to find a wallow, and drowse, and wait. I scratched with my four feet, I crapped, I rolled around, making a nice oblong hole full of startled worms and the delicate fronds of wolf's-claw mosses. Warmed up, the soil began to steam around me; I lay down, resting my muzzle on my front hooves, and dirt lumps cascaded onto my back. I stayed there a long time. The rising sun caressed my snout. I inhaled the passing of the Moon as it dropped down to the other side of the Earth, sending through the night a wind with the tang of chilly sands. It was the thought of Yvan that roused me. Pain flooded back into my belly, and I came round. Frightened of losing myself completely, the way I'd lost Yvan, I tried hard to stand upright. That hurt. It was very difficult to go on without Yvan. It was easier to let myself go: eating and sleeping didn't require much effort, just a little vital force, and there was enough of that in my sow's brain and vulva and brawn to wallow through life. I flopped back into my hole. With my entire body I felt once again the spinning of the planet. I breathed with the shifting winds, my heart beat with the surging tides, and my blood flowed like a torrent of melting snows. I flexed my muscles in communion with trees, odours, mosses, ferns, and rotting leaves. I felt the rallying cry of the animal kingdom course through my body – the ritual combats of the mating season, the musky aroma of my race in a rut. A craving for life sent shivers through me, engulfed me; it was like wild boars galloping in my brain, lightning streaking through my sinews, something that came from the depths of the wind, from the most ancient of bloodlines. I felt in the very fibres of my being the anguish of the dinosaurs, the tenacity of coelacanths, and knowing that these big fish were still alive impelled me to go on – I don't know how to explain it, now, and I don't even know any more how I know all that. Don't laugh. These days, everything in my head is hazy again. I haven't been able to forget Yvan. With each Moon, he reappears in the sky; with each full Moon as round as a belly, I sink back into the pain of my love for Yvan; with each Moon, the sow rises to her feet and weeps. That's why I write: it's because I remain myself through my sorrow over Yvan. Even when I'm in the forest with the other pigs, they often sniff me suspiciously, sensing that human thoughts are still going on in there. I'm unable to rise to their expectations. I don't conform enough to porcine discipline, yet I'm the one who routed the chief danger that threatened them. After I'd heaved myself out of my hole (thanks to the sun, which was well overhead and urging me onwards, in a way), after I'd put those intoxicating smells out of my mind and managed to land on my feet, so to speak, I set off for my mother's house. I was completely unprepared for what I found there. My mother had set up a little farm, with cows, chickens, and pigs. She was obviously making heaps of money now: she had a sparkling new BMW, the farm had its own water-recycling unit, and the SPA logo was all over the place – on the multi-storeyed barn, the sophisticated abattoir, the scrupulously clean rabbit hutch. I strolled around incognito. Several pigs rooting freely in the mud came over to sniff at me, and it was a pleasure to see how well fed they looked. I hid in the cow barn and showered in the spray rinse from the state-of-the-art milking machines. Even though I was born in Garenne-le-Mouillé, I felt perfectly at home in the barn. I smelled faintly of bovine disinfectant, but thanks to a pair of overalls I found hanging on a nail and a huge amount of willpower, I looked human again. I think it was only the thought of Yvan that drove me on. I wanted to ask my mother if it was money or me she wanted, because I had to find out, once and for all, if Yvan had been right about her before he died. My mother welcomed me with open arms in spite of my aroma of cow disinfectant, and she asked how Yvan was doing. My mother hadn't changed; she just seemed a little more tired than before, but she was also happier, stouter, more herself. She'd certainly got a bit of her own back from life with this farm. I told her that Yvan was dead. She said I'd changed terribly, she'd hardly recognized me. She asked me what I planned to do now that Yvan was dead, and whether he'd left me anything. I realized it was useless to continue. I stood up. My mother told me that I was clearly just as dumb as ever, that at least I could have feathered my nest instead of letting myself be plucked clean. She also told me that if I was really in a hole, she could fire the farm girl and take me on at half the minimum wage plus room and board, as there was room in the barn. She offered me coffee. I left without a word because I was no longer able to speak. It did me good to go back to the pigsty, where I could let myself go. I lay down and couldn't even manage to wonder what would become of me. My head was swimming with a rich, pleasing bouquet of smells. A few pigs came in and snuffled at me, some big hogs I thought were rather nice and a large pregnant sow who went to sulk in a corner when she saw me. Cheered by their strong, natural odour, I sort of snuggled down in it, and I snuggled down into my huge, reassuring body surrounded by other huge, reassuring bodies. That smell protected me from everything, it was part of the heart of me. I had, in a way, come home. I was startled when my mother arrived to feed the pigs, and she was startled to find an extra sow. She kicked me to make me turn over, and she sniffed at me, too, and then she smiled a peculiar little smile. When she closed the door – click clack! – the atmosphere became charged with tension. There was so much distress in the air it was almost palpable, it was upsetting everything, I couldn't get to sleep. My companions were all restless, and their good honest smell turned sour, full of bad hormones and stress. The odour separated into distinct zones around individual pigs, as snouts poked around corners, the bottoms of doors, seeking a gap through which to escape, each pig trying to leave every other pig stewing in its own smell of fear. Realizing that the herd would sacrifice its weakest member, I began to quake all over. And to think, real fast, trying to regain my human form, but I was too panicky to concentrate. With my whole pig's body, I could feel and hear the wheels of that truck coming to get us: it was still far away, but speeding along, eating up the road. So we had to be like monkeys, or clever dogs, and solve the problem on our own. It was one of the hogs that found the solution – pigs are quite intelligent, too. But he didn't know what to do with it once he'd found it. Raising his snout towards the door, he stared at the bolt. That's when I remembered the existence of keyholes, locks, and other latches, and the lesson of the refrigerated truck: doors that seem shut tight can still be opened. I went over to the door, shoving the others aside, while my human shape struggled to free itself from my porcine one and pull itself together within me. I saw my right front hoof tremble and grow more slender as tendons went crazy beneath the skin, but nothing popped out, not even one fingertip. I tried to shift that rotten bolt with my hoof, with my snout, but I couldn't, my body didn't understand why it was supposed to work desperately at that piece of steel. My body was moving sluggishly, halfheartedly, whereas every neuron I had was getting in a frazzle trying to keep my mind on one idea: the bolt, the bolt. It's exhausting to wrestle with yourself like that. Something helped me: the scent of a distant perfume. Yerling for Men. It was drawing nearer, with the truck. I was able to stand up. That scent brought back memories of my earlier life, of Perfumes Plus, and the director of the firm. From deep inside me, where it had been hidden for a long, long time, came a surge of revulsion: the director had been wearing this perfume on the day of my job interview. I tried to unbolt the door. Seeing me half transformed like that, my companions began to squeal, almost forgetting about the rumbling of the approaching truck. I heard my mother's footsteps as she left her kitchen and headed for the piggery. That dropped me back onto all fours. Now I was just one big heaving mass of terror. An odour of stainless steel clung to my mother as she approached, a keen determination, something inexorable in the air, and things began to stink horribly of death. The pigs ran every which way inside that pen and I was soundly trampled. I wasn't used to those terrified stampedes yet. Now I know that even during the mildest cloudburst, extreme concentration is required to stay calm, to resist the gut-wrenching panic that seizes our vitals, the dread animals have felt ever since the very first thunderstorm. It's the same with death. Death was all around me, and I had to keep my head. Huddling in a corner behind the other frightened pigs, I saw the door open. The truck arrived at that moment, parked in front of the door, and out stepped the director of Perfumes Plus. He had grown enormously fat and looked as strong as an ox. I watched as, framed in the doorway, he leaned down to kiss my mother on the mouth and squeeze her rear end with a certain tenderness. The name on the truck was Welfare Electronics, but it reeked of carcasses in there. The director and my mother were supplying the black market, and with the high price of meat these days, they must have been making a bloody fortune. The director was dressed like a business executive, but my mother gave him a white apron and a rope, and the two of them entered the pen. My mother was holding a large knife, a copper basin to catch the blood, and some newspaper for singeing the skin. 'Over there, in the back,' she said. She put down the basin and newspaper. They came towards me. The other pigs fled with great pushing and shoving, leaving a big empty circle around me. I prepared to sell my life dearly.

Besides being a murderer, my mother was a thief; she was going to kill a pig that didn't belong to her. I bared my teeth, and the director laughed. He tossed the rope over me. All that last scene with Yvan came back to me, surging into my brain, my belly, my muscles, and I stood up to my full height, full of hatred, full of fear, I don't know – full of my love for Yvan, perhaps. The director turned green. When he pulled a revolver from his pocket, I tore the gun from his shaking hands. I fired twice: first at him, then at my mother. The knife clattered into the copper basin. Afterwards I went off into the forest. Some of the pigs followed me, while the others, too attached to the comforts of their modern pigsty, were probably taken away by the SPA or by another farmer, but in any case, I wouldn't want to be in their place today.

Now I'm a sow most of the time. It's more convenient for life in the forest. I've taken up with a very handsome, very virile wild boar. In the evening, I often return to the farm. That's where I stole this notebook. I watch television. I phoned the director's mother. I've observed everything from the woods, ever since the day the crew from *Vanished Without a Trace* showed up. They found my prints on the revolver lying next to the bodies, and the ratings meter is about to explode. But they can go on looking for me for ever, at this point. I'm not unhappy with my lot. The food's good, the clearing comfortable, the young wild boars are entertaining. I often relax and enjoy myself. There's nothing better than warm earth around you when you wake up in the morning, the smell of your own body mingling with the odour of humus, the first mouthfuls you take without even getting up, gobbling acorns, chestnuts, everything that has rolled down into the wallow while you were scrabbling in your dreams. I write whenever my animal spirits subside a little. The mood comes over me when the Moon rises, and I reread my notebook in its cold light. I try to do what Yvan taught me, but for the opposite reason: when I crane my neck towards the Moon, it's to show, once again, a human face.